CUSTOMER SERVICE EXCELLENCE

Libraries & Archives

Kent
County
Council

00884\DTP\RN\07.07   LIB 7

THE HOUSE OF SECRETS

Jean Davidson

CHIVERS

British Library Cataloguing in Publication Data available

This Large Print edition published by AudioGO Ltd, Bath, 2010.
Published by arrangement with the author.

U.K. Hardcover ISBN 978 1 408 49275 8
U.K. Softcover ISBN 978 1 408 49276 5

Printed and bound in Great Britain by
CPI Antony Rowe, Chippenham and Eastbourne

CHAPTER ONE

Laura looked out of the railway station doorway across the yard. Empty. Has he forgotten me, she thought? A gust of wind blew heavy driving rain towards her and she stepped hastily back into the safety of the station hall. If I don't look at the clock for another—oh, five minutes—then someone will arrive, she told herself. She looked up at the big dusty clock on the wall. In the hissing gaslight she read that it was ten minutes past six. Surely her new employer hadn't forgotten when she was arriving? She'd written the time clearly in her letter of confirmation last week.

In the silence she could hear the creaking of the station signs as they were rocked by the wind, and the rattle as one of the milk churns she'd seen standing on the platform waiting for collection, was knocked over. She guessed it couldn't have had milk in it.

When she had followed the two other passengers who'd also descended at Hamholt Halt into the station hallway, she'd encountered the stationmaster, a rotund little man with grey hair curling from under his uniform hat and a cheerful twinkle in his eye. He'd greeted the other passengers, now long gone, by name and then taken her ticket, read it carefully, casting glances of curiosity her

1

way.

'All the way from London today,' he'd said. 'It's a long journey. Want a conveyance ordering?'

'No—no thanks, I'm being met,' she'd said, feeling herself redden guiltily, looking down so that the rim of her bonnet would hide her face.

'You can wait for 'en in my office. It's warm in there,' he'd offered. 'I've just brewed some tea.' Over which he'd try to pump her for information about who she was and where she was going. She couldn't allow that.

'They might be waiting for me already, or just coming,' she'd replied, pushing past him. 'But thank you sir.'

Only there hadn't been a conveyance waiting for her. All she saw was creeping twilight, arriving early because of the thick grey clouds overhead and the rain that sheeted from them. Beyond the station yard which was enclosed by white painted rails, she saw the road led to a cluster of houses. Hamholt, she'd supposed. No one was visible in the street. Light flickered dimly in a couple of windows.

She glanced up at the clock: twelve minutes past six. She couldn't stop herself; she looked outside again. Nothing. Nobody.

The last of her bravado drained away. What have I done, she thought, as the hard fact of her flight from everyone and everything she'd known all her life, suddenly hit her. She was tired, hungry, cold and alone. And had very

2

little money. She was in a strange county, hundreds of miles from anyone who knew her.

She felt a lump form in her throat and swallowed hard. No. She was not going to start feeling sorry for herself. This was what she'd chosen to do and she had to go through with it.

She sniffed and felt in her jacket pocket for her handkerchief. As she blew her nose and dabbed at her eyes, her resolve strengthened. She could not have stayed, not in those circumstances. She'd had no option but to find some means of escape. There had been no one she could turn to for help. So she'd helped herself, even though she'd hated being secretive one minute, and then terrified of discovery or not getting away in time, the next. And she'd managed it. She was here now.

In the next moment a horse and cart swung into the yard, a candle glimmering in the one carriage lamp. The farm cart was pulled by a brown and white carthorse with a shaggy mane, and there was a lone driver. He pulled up outside the station entrance and jumped down.

'Miss Laura Crestwood? I'm sorry to be late. This cursed storm brought a tree down in the lane and I had to get Tom out to help move it.'

He stepped to the door, pulled off a leather glove and held out his hand. Without thinking she took it and as they shook hands he lifted his wide brimmed hat. She saw a strong jaw, brown eyes and dark tousled hair before he settled it back on his head.

'You are Mr Colefax?'

'Yes, and welcome to Hamholt, Devon. Did you have a good journey?'

'Yes, thank you.' All the petty annoyances of the many hours of travel were fading already.

'Is this yours?' he picked up her carpet bag. 'There's a tarpaulin in the back. It'll be dry under there and so will you.' A brief smile touched his lips. 'You'd better get used to the rain. Devon is known for it.'

He helped her up the step into the back of the cart, where she settled herself and her bag under the tarpaulin. It made for a cold, clammy cloak, but he was right, it was dry underneath. She lifted it so that it covered her bonnet too.

Colefax climbed up nimbly and made clicking noises to encourage the horse forward, turning the cart expertly out of the yard and into the road beyond. Just for a moment she had a sense that the stationmaster's nose was pressed up against the window of his warm office, eager to see who had picked up the stranger from London. But when she looked across, she couldn't see him.

Colefax turned the cart to the left at the end of the rise and gee'ed the horse into a trot. Soon Laura was aware of nothing but the roaring and tossing of trees and bushes which first topped high banks on either side of the

4

lane and then gave way to flat woodland. The lamp gave only just enough light to see the broad back and shoulders of her employer—her first employer—intent on keeping the cart moving forward at a steady pace, and no doubt alert for fallen branches or sudden pools in the lane.

There was no point in trying to talk. Neither could have heard the other above the noise of the storm. The wind and rain stung her eyes so she had to keep blinking to see anything at all. What a contrast to this morning, she thought. The clip and rattle of hackney carriages and drays, the occasional rumble of a motor vehicle, the smart London streets, passers-by in their finery and latest fashions. She felt a bubble of laughter, and put her hand over her mouth to quieten it, as her shoulders shook. I must be very tired, she thought, or light-headed with the strangeness of it all. Just think, the young Miss Crestwood in the back of a cart under a sack, alone in the night with a young—well, youngish, she wasn't quite sure of his age yet—man. She could hear the outraged tones of their elderly neighbour: "The young women of today don't know the meaning of the word ladylike."

After a while she raised her head. The wind seemed to be dying down and the rain easing off. She pulled the wet tarpaulin away from her head and let it settle on her shoulders. They were still in woodland but the trees were

5

thinning out.

And then she saw her. A child standing on the grass verge dressed in a white shift. Her long hair was plastered wetly to her head. She stared at Laura as the cart passed by but didn't call out.

Laura took hold of Colefax's arm. 'Stop,' she shouted above the howl of the wind. 'Please stop.'

The cart came to a halt and he turned round. 'Is something the matter? What's happened?'

'There's a little girl—look!'

Laura pointed back the way they'd come. But there was no small child standing by the roadside.

'A little girl?' Colefax was concerned. 'Is she hurt? Whereabouts did you see her?' He picked up the lantern and held it aloft. Laura stood up and steadied herself with a hand on the side of the cart and they looked around.

'I'm sorry,' she said after a few moments. 'I can't see her anywhere. She couldn't have disappeared that quickly, you can see through the trees here.'

'No, there's no one there,' he agreed. 'Perhaps it was mist. It's easy to imagine all sorts of things on a night like this. Unless it was a Devon piskey.' He grinned. 'We're nearly home now anyway. See, there's the driveway entrance.'

A few paces ahead a narrow drive led off to

the right, curving away between huge rhododendron bushes, some with their flowers open. Laura sat down again and the cart moved off, the horse pricking its ears up at the sight of its stable.

Laura glanced behind her again. A little girl couldn't have run away that fast. Colefax was right. She must have imagined her.

The driveway curved to the left. Laura squinted over Brendan Colefax's shoulder, blinking the last of the raindrops that ran down from her damp bonnet, from her eyes. At last she could make out the shape of the building. Barton Court was the address she'd written to, but although a good size it was not the imposing manor house she'd been expecting. Nor were there any welcoming lights in the windows. In the flickering light of the carriage lamp and the last light of day she could just make out rough grey stone walls and a slate roof.

'Miss Crestwood,' her new employer said as he pulled the horse to a stop. 'I'll leave you here while I see to Champion. Give the bell a good pull, and Mrs Hannacott will let you in.'

He jumped down then moved to the back of the cart and held out his hand to help her down. As she put her foot on the step her boot slipped on the wet wood and to keep her balance she put her hand on Colefax's shoulder to steady herself. He felt firm and muscular under his coat. She quickly moved her hand, relieved that he made no comment, but lifted down her bag.

'There's the porch. As I said, the bell is a bit stiff so don't be gentle with it.'

'Thank you.'

She looked after him as he led Champion and the cart around the back of Barton Court, speaking to the horse and rubbing its nose. For the first time a trickle of doubt entered her mind. Brendan Colefax had driven to collect her himself, and now appeared to be acting as groom and stable boy too. If he could not afford staff other than Mrs Hannacott would he be able to afford her salary on top of her board and lodging? Was everything as she expected it to be?

She decided she was too tired to make any sense of it. All she wanted was to get beside a warm fire and have something to eat and drink. Tomorrow morning would be time enough to take stock. At least, she had to hope so.

Her wet boots chafed her ankles as she went into the stone porch. She had to grope over the stone with her fingers till she felt the handle of the bell pull and gave it a strong yank. She couldn't hear the answering ring, and was about to pull again when she heard the rattle of the door being unlocked.

'Whatever for did Master Colefax send you to the front? I don't know,' Mrs Hannacott was saying before she'd even opened the door

8

fully. 'Come along in. You must be froze, young Miss.'

'Laura Crestwood.' She smiled and held out her hand without thinking. Mrs Hannacott looked at it then took it gingerly for a moment in her left hand. In her right she carried an oil lamp, its comforting glow making Laura blink after the dark.

'Pleased to meet you, Miss,' she said. Laura found she was looking down at a head of fair hair streaked with grey, wound up in a big bun and adorned with a small lace cap. Her round features were flushed, her brown eyes bright and curious. She wore a large apron over her ample curves. She in turn cast assessing eyes over Laura.

She turned a large iron key in the front door behind them then led the way down the hall. It was clearly unused. Cobwebs hung from the ceiling and their steps echoed on bare stone flags. There were no pictures on the walls. Laura's trickle of doubt returned, this time as a river of concern. Would she even have a bed in her bedroom?

Mrs Hannacott led her through a gloomy parlour. She had an impression of a few hulking pieces of furniture, but she didn't linger to look. She hurried on to get away from the musty smell of damp and neglect. Then there was a short stone passageway and finally they entered the kitchen. Laura took in a deep breath of fresh air filled with the smell of food.

Her stomach rumbled in response.

'Isn't it bright and warm,' she blurted out, relieved that there was at least one habitable room in Barton Court. Mrs Hannacott cast her a look that said she understood exactly what Laura meant.

Another oil lamp gleamed from a wooden dresser, and candles burned on the scrubbed wooden table in the centre of the room, on the mantel, and a black range also cast extra light. On the rag rug in front of the range a large orange and white cat was curled up seemingly asleep. Then one large topaz eye opened, examined her, and closed again. Was it as good at catching mice as sleeping, she wondered.

Three place settings of blue and white striped pottery ware were laid on the table. In the centre was a breadboard carrying a big loaf of bread and beside it a bread-knife.

'I've a hot stew ready for you on such a night. Not really May fare, but it's something colder than it ought to be,' the little woman said. 'Master allowed for a fire to be lit in your bedroom above, to air it. The necessary is out there through the scullery and you can wash your hands in the scullery sink and when you come back you can cut the bread while I serve the stew. Take a candle with you.'

Laura took a candlestick from the mantel-shelf. The house didn't even have gas laid on, she thought and shivered in the chill air of the scullery as she moved swiftly through to the necessary, trying not to see yet more spiders' webs high on the walls.

As she was washing her hands in cold water over a deep stone sink using rough washing soap, the scullery door opened and Brendan Colefax entered, in the process of rolling up his sleeves. He nodded to her.

'Mrs Hannacott's made us a fine supper,' he said as he waited for her to finish.

She dried her hands quickly on a harsh towel, feeling awkward at being closeted with this strange man in a confined space. But it was something she would have to get used to.

'Is the horse—Champion—all right?' she enquired politely.

He gave her an amused look. 'Yes, I've rubbed him down and he's already tucking into his hay.'

Laura hurried out of the scullery. Now she had to face the task of carving bread, not something she'd had to do before. She grasped the bread and the knife firmly and sawed diligently. Both she and Mrs Hannacott stared at the uneven results. Although the housekeeper said nothing, Laura was sure she'd marked it down. But, she told herself, how would Mrs Hannacott be on her handwriting and typewriting?

'Sit you down and pour yourself some water or cider while I dish up.'

Mrs Hannacott's strong arms made light work of carrying the big iron pan to the table

11

and then she ladled the stew onto their plates. So they were all eating together! No separate servants' hall. Once again Laura pictured this morning in the parlour. The rustle of a newspaper, the chink of fine bone china and the curtsey of the maid before she cleared their plates away. She'd entered an entirely new world. A brave new world, perhaps.

'Grace, Miss Crestwood?'

She came to, and realised that Brendan Colefax was also now seated at the table. She bowed her head as he said a simple grace. It was impossible to concentrate. Her mind teemed with so many questions and now she added another. As her employer spoke she detected a slight accent. Was it Scottish? Northern? It was quite different to the housekeeper's broad Devon. But now was not the time for conversation, polite or otherwise. They each concentrated on eating and confined themselves to discussing the food, the home-made bread, the weather. There was a complicated discussion about which local stream had burst its banks and which fields, all named, were flooded. Over a dessert of apple pie and clotted cream—Laura watched in awe at her first sight of the rich cream melting over the hot pie—Brendan Colefax and Mrs Hannacott fell to discussing the local village, and in particular she heard them mention a man called Parr.

'He'm at it again,' Mrs Hannacott said.

'Tom heard him clear as day, stirring it up in the Church House Inn.'

'We'll have to hope that time will mellow him,' Colefax said, frowning and it seemed the cares of the world had settled on his shoulders. Tactfully Mrs Hannacott changed the subject to the next day's menu.

Suddenly Laura realised that her eyelids had started drooping, and she could no longer concentrate. The warmth, the feeling of being full, the cider too, on top of the long day's travel, were making her sleepy.

'Miss Crestwood, I think I should show you your room,' Colefax said. 'No, don't get up Mrs Hannacott. Rest that ankle some more, you can leave the kitchen door open for propriety. She wrenched it coming down the stairs earlier,' he explained to Laura.

'But we haven't discussed our work,' she said, forcing herself upright again and her eyes wide open. She didn't object to a man showing her her bedroom. This was another world where the rules no longer applied.

'Plenty of time for that tomorrow morning,' he said. 'Follow me—and yes, I will have another helping of pie when I come down, Mrs Hannacott.'

He picked up Laura's cloak, which had been steaming in front of the fire, and her bag, and took a lamp in his other hand. As she followed him back into the stone passageway then through another door and up a flight of stairs

13

she had a further impression of decay, of cracked and crumbling plasterwork, of creaking floors and the sense of a house long unused.

'This is your room, above the kitchen so it should benefit from the warmth.' He lifted the latch in a plain wooden door and led the way in. The walls and sloping roof were limewashed and flower sprigged cotton curtains hung at the small window. There was a tiny grate with the embers of a fire behind a stout fireguard. One big brass bedstead heaped with down comforter and blankets and a wooden washstand bearing a china bowl and matching jug, were the only furniture.

'There are some hooks on the wall for you to hang your clothes.' Brendan Colefax gestured to the wall. 'I daresay we'll find a chest of drawers somewhere fit for you to use.'

He put down her belongings, raised the lamp and then looked at her properly. She saw that his eyes were a dark blue, and in the clear light of the lamp she saw that he was younger than she had thought. Perhaps not yet thirty?

'I shall be across the yard. I sleep in the laboratory, but Mrs Hannacott will be downstairs, next to the kitchen. If you are—alarmed at all—in the night—call out. We will hear you.'

'There are—just the three of us here?' she asked.

'Just the three of us. I realise that these are

somewhat unorthodox circumstances. Perhaps rather different to what you are used to.'

His gaze was searching. She could not risk his finding out just how inexperienced she was, not at this early stage before she'd had a chance to prove herself. If she probed further now, then so might he. It looked as if they both had something to hide.

She lifted her chin. 'I shall enjoy the challenge,' she replied.

She met his gaze again. Whatever he saw seemed to satisfy him for after a moment he gave a nod. 'Good night and sleep well Miss Crestwood. We won't worry about time-keeping on your first day. Come down when you're ready tomorrow.'

He gave a brief smile, making his serious features seem even younger, then was gone.

She had just enough firelight to see to hang up her two changes of clothes, a neat plaid suit for everyday, and a black dress for more formal wear. She hoped the creases would fall out and the hooks not make a mark. She'd not have anyone to hang and press her garments now. She left her underclothes in her bag, and placed her toiletries on the washstand, then looked around for somewhere to put her jewellery box and two books. She pulled aside the curtains and found a deep window seat and for the first time felt she'd found a place of her own. Somewhere to sit and read, and write. Though she only had one person she could write to.

As she lay in her bed, ignoring the lumps in the mattress, feet tucked on the stone hot water bottle wrapped in flannel, nightgown pulled warmly around her, she listened to the howl of the wind in the chimney and the rattle of raindrops on the windowpanes as another squall came in. So many questions whirled in her mind. Why hadn't she asked when she'd get paid? She had little money left after buying her ticket and food on the journey. And what were her hours to be and where exactly would she be working?

And this house? Surely it wasn't her new employer's family home as she'd originally assumed? Why was it so rundown? And why was he sleeping in the laboratory? He'd said she was to call out if frightened—what could happen to frighten her? And what was that villager, Parr, stirring up?

There was no point in worrying now, she decided, especially as to whether she'd landed herself in a worse position than she one she'd left behind. At last she felt sleep arriving. Her last thought was of the small child in the road, and her beseeching eyes.

CHAPTER TWO

Laura pulled aside the cotton curtain and knelt on the window seat. It was covered by a thin fold of linen and she could feel the rough stone underneath pressing into her knees. The windowpanes were smeared with dust and dirt and so, to see better, she lifted the catch and managed to open the small window with a couple of shoves of her palm.

She caught her breath. She looked at a completely different world to the one she'd seen yesterday. The sky was blue and the sun warm. Beyond the farmyard and outbuildings was a steep, rounded hill of pastureland speckled with buttercups and daisies. Hedges ran down the hill, decorated with may blossom. On top of the hill was a small copse.

Everywhere she looked was green and lush, the sunlight glittering in dewdrops. From somewhere she could hear the cawing of crows. Apart from Barton Court Farm it seemed they were alone in the world. I've never been so far from other buildings and rushing crowds, she thought.

A movement caught her attention and she was surprised to see a beautifully groomed bay horse, bridled and saddled, flicking flies away with its well-combed black tail. A far cry from the homely shaggy carthorse Champion who'd

17

pulled them home last night. Home? Was she calling it that so soon?

As she leaned forward for a better view the wooden door to one of the outbuildings opened and a young man stepped out. She saw from the cut of his coat and trousers that he was wearing the latest London fashion of that spring. He was clean shaven, his black hair smooth and also fashionably cut. He was as handsome and well groomed as his horse. She decided it must be his.

Brendan Colefax appeared in the doorway behind him. He was wearing brown corduroy trousers, and an old leather jerkin over a white shirt with its sleeves rolled up. He appeared to be scowling, in contrast with the stranger's jaunty grin. The stranger turned and said something to him, received a curt nod in reply, then jammed his hat on his head and in one fluid movement mounted his horse.

As he wheeled his horse away he looked straight up at Laura in the open window. She gasped and pulled her head in quickly, bumping it on the wooden frame. Had he really seen her or had she just imagined that he'd tipped his hat to her, eyes twinkling?

And had Colefax seen her? She ventured to look down again, but he had gone back inside. That must be the laboratory where he worked—and slept at night. It bordered one side of the empty farmyard, a single storey stone building. On another side was an empty hay barn and stables, and opposite the farmhouse was a fence and barred gate that led to the green hillside.

Dismissing the handsome stranger from her mind she closed the window and began to wash in cold water at the washstand. She had slept very deeply and still felt muzzy after all her travelling the day before. If there had been something to alarm me, she thought recalling Colefax's words of the night before, I wouldn't have heard it anyway.

She took her plaid dress from the hook on the wall, hung up her outfit from yesterday, then began to pull on her clothes, struggling with the fastenings. What would be happening back in London now? When would they first realise that she was gone? Surely last night, when she hadn't returned from the friend she'd said she'd gone to visit. Servants would have been sent out, enquiries made. Maybe at first they'd think it was an act of pique or defiance.

But now—would they have sent for the police? As she put her fob watch in place and began to comb her hair her mind began to race. Would they hire a private detective? Thank goodness Sherlock Holmes, whose adventures were all the rage in London, was not real or he'd probably have tracked her down by now.

A thought struck her. The stranger talking to Colefax—nothing to do with her, was it?

Surely not, this early on. She mustn't let her anxieties run away with her. But had she done the right thing, not leaving a letter of explanation? She intended, somehow, to let them know later on that she was safe and the reason why she'd left.

She peered into the small broken mirror on the wall and began the struggle to put up her long brown hair by herself, no maid to help her today. Brown hair, blue eyes, she thought, very commonplace and not so easy to trace. Drat, it was harder to put her hair in place than she'd expected. But as she worked at it she felt a sudden exhilaration. She was free! Now all she had to do was please Brendan Colefax with her work. Further ahead than that, she refused to think.

She pushed open the door to the kitchen, filled with anticipation at the breakfast that might be awaiting her. Or would she be expected to make her own? And would there be tea or coffee this deep in the country?

Her cheerful, 'Good morning Mrs Hannacott,' died on her lips at the sight of another strange man, this one considerably older and wearing working clothes and solid boots. He was standing by the back door, holding a mug in his hand. Mrs Hannacott was standing close in front of him, hand on the back of a chair to support her. They were so deep in conversation, neither noticed Laura.

She made a big show of closing the kitchen

20

door, rattling the latch loudly. Mrs Hannacott
and the man sprang apart. He cleared his
throat noisily. 'Reckon I'll be off then. Thanks
for the tea, Amy.'

'Mind how you go, Tom,' Mrs Hannacott
replied.

So that was Tom. But before she could
thank him for clearing the road during the
storm the previous night, he'd gone through
the back door, giving her only a cursory glance.

'Sleep well, Miss?' Mrs Hannacott asked,
nodding at a chair to indicate she should sit
down. On the table was the remains of the
bread from last night, a slab of cheese, butter
on a plate, and an unlabelled jar of jam.

'Yes thank you, like a log. What a beautiful
morning.'

'To some, maybe,' was her curious reply.
'Help yourself. That's my sister's home-made
rhubarb jam. Dab hand at it, she is. There's
tea in the pot on the hob, or make some fresh
if you want. If you're after coffee, you'll have
to ask Mr Colefax to order some at the village
stores.' She refused to meet Laura's gaze as
she spoke, pouring tea from a large brown pot
with a chipped spout and banging it down on
the table. 'When you're done, Master Colefax
says to go and join him in the 'boratory. Now,
I've got jobs to be getting on with.' And she
disappeared through the door to the scullery,
still limping.

As yesterday, she wore a black gown, pintucked and buttoned down the front, and now a lace cap over her hair. In the daylight Laura noticed more grey in her fair hair. How long did it take her to put her hair in that bun or did she sleep like it? What concerned her more, though, was Mrs Hannacott's furtive behaviour. Perhaps she was annoyed at being interrupted in a tryst? Or maybe this was her usual way.

Ignoring the clattering sounds from the scullery she poured milk into her tea and drank some of the well-stewed brew, then helped herself to bread, cheese and jam. It all tasted wonderful. How strange to be eating alone—apart from a few pestering flies—with nothing but birdsong in the distance. No street vendor cries, rattling cabs and carts and horses' hooves.

When she finished she tidied away as best she could, wiped her hands on the cloth airing on the range, then went outside.

A light breeze ruffled the creamy cow parsley and long grasses around the edge of the neglected farmyard. Already the sun's heat was strong, sucking moisture out of the ground. She headed for the door she'd seen Colefax standing at earlier on, then hesitated. Should she knock? Perhaps it would be a good idea.

She noticed her fingers were trembling and acknowledged for the first time how nervous she felt. Would she be able to do the job she claimed she could do? Would she be able to understand what was being asked of her? Or would the long journey turn out to be a waste of time and she would have to leave.

Come on Laura, she chided herself, what would Aunt Rose say? I can't let her down. So she knocked and went in.

The walls and ceiling of the long stone building had been completely whitewashed, while the stone-flagged floor had been brushed clean of dust and debris. Along the centre of the room trestle tables had been set up and on these stood a bewildering array of glass and brass scientific instruments, including a large microscope, gas jets and rubber tubing, and brass weighing scales. There were also large casks of different coloured liquids, some marked 'Danger'.

'Ah, Miss Crestwood.' Brendan Colefax had been concentrating on filling a flask from one of the larger casks. He put it down carefully and came over to her. In the clearer light of day she saw how his thick brown hair held a glint of gold, and that there were shadows under his eyes. Where did he sleep out here? Not on the floor, surely?

'Do you have everything you need? Were you comfortable last night?' he asked, studying her face much as she had been studying his.

'I've just had a very good breakfast and thank you, I slept really well.' She paused. Now was not the time to ask about coffee.

'And you?' she asked, then realised that she was an employee and this wasn't a polite exchange in a drawing-room. Would he notice her inappropriate remark?

He gave the glimmer of a smile. 'Nothing could have kept me awake after battling that storm,' he said. 'But the weather looks set fair now.'

'It's beautiful here—what a morning. And not another house in sight!' Really, what was wrong with her, talking in this breathless way? She was an employee. He was her employer.

'It's not far to the nearest village, Manleigh. About half an hour on foot if you go over the hill and then join the lane.'

'Is it a big village?'

'There's a pub and a provisions store and some other shops. Mrs Hannacott fetches what we need.' He hesitated. "I don't go into the village much myself. I fetch goods I've ordered by train, or go into Bovey—Bovey Tracey. One or two of the villagers haven't taken kindly to a stranger in their midst.' He smiled ruefully. 'Mrs Hannacott says to give them time, they'll come round. They haven't taken against her for working here, so you should be accepted.'

Laura nodded. It seemed she'd stumbled on a sore point. But before she could probe further he said, 'Now to work. Your hands, are they clean?'

She held them out for inspection, like a child. 'I wiped them on a towel after

24

breakfast.'

He shook his head. 'We have to avoid any kind of contamination. Nothing must be introduced except by our own choosing. I may occasionally need you to help me, so please scrub your hands at the sink.'

'I see, Mr Colefax,' she said demurely.

He cast her a glance. 'What do you know about medical science Miss Crestwood?'

'I read the newspapers.'

'That's a start. There's so much going on in the field. Nearly every week brings a major advance. We're achieving so much in reducing human suffering, and getting to the bottom of what causes disease. As well as finding cures. I'm hoping to add to that knowledge with what I'm doing here.'

His brown eyes were lit by the passion of his words. 'However, while I understand science, and medicine, I'm no good at record-keeping. And in order to present findings, all studies must be written up well. That's where you come in.'

'I'll try my best,' she said, daunted by the importance of what he was doing, and keeping her greasy hands tight by her side till she could wash them. 'Where shall I work?'

He nodded to two doors at the side of the room. 'The door on the left is where I sleep, the one on the right is the office. I need you to take control of the paper in there and to type up my notes. Are you ready?'

'As soon as I've washed my hands.' She gritted her teeth. This was it!

The 'office' had a small window opening on to the farmyard, a desk, a chair and typewriter—and lots of paper files, box files, piles of notebooks. They were heaped on the floor and on the single shelf fixed to the wall. Brendan ran his hands through his hair and gestured apologetically. 'I've tried to keep them in date order, but sometimes when I've tried to look something up, it takes me forever to find, so everything is out of sequence.'

'But you have dated everything?' He nodded. 'Then I'm sure I'll be able to find it.' She noticed a framed certificate on the otherwise bare, whitewashed walls. 'Is that yours?'

'Yes.' For some reason he stared at it gloomily. 'My physician's certificate from Edinburgh University.'

'So why did you choose to come here, to Devon? Wouldn't it have been easier to work in a lab in Edinburgh, where you're known?'

He looked away. 'I needed to be far away.' He looked back. 'And you?'

'About the same.' Their eyes met and Laura felt a moment of understanding between them. They both had their secrets, and here they could leave the past behind.

'Now let me show you how I've grouped the files,' Brendan Colefax was first to break the silence.

After half an hour's explanations her head was spinning, and then thankfully he left her to make a start. She placed the first files on the desk, then touched the keys of the typewriter. It was a big black metal Imperial. She'd learned on one of those. It had a heavy action, but it was solid and reliable.

As she went to fetch some white paper she glanced at the certificate again. 'Brendan Colefax Esq., surgeon, summa cum laude. 1886'. Top honours then. And a surgeon. Why wasn't he practising as a surgeon now? The most highly paid and respected of positions. Another thought struck her. Who was funding his research?

She put aside speculation about money and her employer for the time being. First she had to conquer the Imperial.

*   *   *

'. . . and so, dearest Aunt Rose, I hope you'll be pleased that all those hours of typewriting lessons you paid for have proved useful in the end. I can't say I understand much of what I'm typing, and sometimes I have to write chemical formulas by hand, but Mr Colefax seemed happy with the results at the end of the day. Now my fingers are very sore. When I go into the village to post this letter to you I'll look for some ointment.

'I'm sitting in the window seat and outside I

can see bats flying over the farmyard, and the first stars. Mr Colefax is still in his laboratory. I can see lamplight in the windows.

'I think I must have learned a love of adventure from you. I hope you approve—or at least understand—why I've done what I've done. I wait to hear from you, your loving niece, Laura, Devon.'

She cleaned the nib of her pen then placed it in its case, and closed the inkwell. Then, by the light of her candle, she read through the letter. Aunt Rose was the one person in the world, surely, who would show sympathy. If only Aunt Rose hadn't been consumed by wanderlust, spending her time exploring Turkey and the Middle East, collecting plants and making botanical drawings for a book she intended to finish 'one day'.

A powerful and painful memory forced its way into her mind. Aunt Rose facing her in front of the fireplace of home, the house where she'd been born and spent her first nine years. She still could not accept that her mother and father and two brothers really had drowned. Their ship had been on its way to Africa where her father had a civil engineering project.

'I'm so sorry, Laura, that I can't stay here and make a home for you,' Aunt Rose gestured at the cluttered living-room. 'It's just not in me. I'd only be miserable and make you miserable too. I inherited your grandmother's rebellious nature, and a little of her artistic talent. Your mother was always the sensible one.' She reached out and they hugged each other for comfort for a while. 'Our second cousins will be able to give you a settled home, and I'll be watching over you from wherever I am.'

'But I've never met them!'

Aunt Rose sighed. 'Neither have I, but Horace is a banker, and they have offered to take you in. They'll make sure you're brought up well.'

True to her word Aunt Rose had written regularly, however remote her location, with sketches in the margins. Laura had kept all her letters and it had really hurt to leave them behind but she hadn't been able to carry them. Would her second cousins burn them? And her aunt had sent money, insisting that Laura learn the newest secretarial skills. Horace and Venetia Middleship had, even if they couldn't love her, made sure she was fed, clothed and lived comfortably, and she'd not suffered especially at the hands of their four children. It wasn't their fault that she'd felt so stifled. Which made the shock of their betrayal worse. Had this always been their plan? Was that the only reason they'd taken her in?

She blotted the ink, folded the letter, then placed it in the envelope she'd addressed earlier, to her Aunt c/o the British Embassy, Istanbul, then began to prepare for bed. Her heart ached anew for the loss of her parents and her happy early years. She tried not to dwell on the past and what her life might have been like if her parents had lived but every now and then the memories crowded in. She fell asleep with a smile on her lips, reliving that last evening before her parents and older brothers left, an evening of fun and frolics and promises to send for her soon . . .

CHAPTER THREE

Even though the lane to the village was sunk between high banks with shady trees arching high overhead, it was still very hot and humid. Laura was glad to see the first houses of Manleigh Village in view from the top of the next rise. She'd enjoyed the walk from the farm, observing the wild flowers in the hedgerows—she only knew the names of one or two, like foxgloves—and hearing the birdsong. But now she felt hot and uncomfortable in her thick clothes and boots. It had taken her about half an hour she reckoned, hearing the church clock strike ten, hoping it kept accurate time. She had left her fob watch behind in her bedroom. It had belonged to her mother and she didn't want to risk losing it.

The first cottages she passed were a dingy

brown colour. Their thatched rooves were sunken and had patches of grass and weeds growing in them. Small grimy windows gave nothing away. But as she neared the village centre the cottages were more spruce though still needing some paint. She glimpsed one or two stone or brick houses behind hedges and gardens but had the general impression this was a poor village.

At its heart was an open area, in the centre a green with a chestnut tree spreading shade. Laura paused and looked around. She saw the post office immediately, on one corner. Next to it was a general grocery, and on the other side a bank. On the second side was a clothing store, and down a side street she glimpsed a dairy and a forge. And taking up the third side of the square was the Church House Inn, its walls covered in ivy, and already a couple of men were sitting outside with tankards in hand, drinking. There was also a shining bay horse tethered nearby.

A group of four women stood gossiping together outside the clothing store and two older women sat companionably side by side on the seat around the bole of the chestnut tree. Small children played on the grass in front of them. She was aware that all of them were casting her covert glances.

She headed for the post office to send the letter to her Aunt Rose. She had only a few shillings left in all the world, but that would be enough. She also had a shopping list and some money given her by Mrs Hannacott, who had also given her very firm instructions as to what to look for as regards freshness and ripeness, and where to find the items. Just as well, because she'd never shopped for food before, that had always been done by the servants. She was looking forward to the experience.

She'd asked Brendan Colefax for permission to go to the village, expecting him to make her complete several days' work before giving her time off. She'd found him in her office, looking through the work she'd typed the day before.

'This is very good,' he said. 'Seeing it written up properly begins to make me feel as if I'm achieving something here. If you could leave wider margins, that would be helpful in case I want to add extra notes.'

'You'll need to check it over anyway, in case I've made mistakes in the figures. For example here,' she pointed to numbers on the page, her fingers accidentally brushing his. She felt her heart miss a beat, and looked up to find his brown eyes on her, rather than the page.

'What? Oh yes. I'll read everything through very carefully,' he said. They moved away from each other, both aware of their sudden closeness.

'I don't really understand what your experiments are about,' she ventured. 'Would it help?'

He nodded. 'It would. But I'd rather not go into that at the moment. I do have my reasons. Can you trust me on that?' He met her gaze again, and she thought she caught a glimpse of a deeper pain, quickly hidden.

'Of course. Mr Colefax, I've written a letter to my aunt and I'd like to go to the post office some time, would that be all right? I know I've only been here a couple of days and perhaps I'm not due any time off.'

'That's not a problem.' He paused. Was this also his first time as an employer, she wondered. 'I'm afraid I can't spare the horse today, if you don't mind the walk you may as well go now.'

'I'll enjoy it,' she declared.

He flashed her a quick smile. 'And I'm sure Mrs Hannacott will need some supplies, so check with her first.'

'I will. Does anyone round here ride a bicycle? Maybe I could borrow one in the future.'

'I've seen one or two in Bovey Tracey. Can you ride one?'

She thought of her wobbling attempts on her friend's bicycle, but she had succeeded in the end. 'Yes, though there are more hills here than in—where I come from.'

'I first learned on a velocipede, it was so uncomfortable . . .' He went with her, discussing bicycles, to the farmhouse to let Mrs Hannacott know what was happening. He

33

didn't appear to have noticed that she'd avoided saying where in London she'd come from. She'd used a PO Box for their correspondence.

As she approached Manleigh Post Office she had to pass the group of gossiping women. They stared at her openly. What should she do? She wouldn't normally speak to strangers in the street in London, but it might be different here.

'Good morning,' she said and heard a muttered response. She felt that four pairs of eyes were glued to her back and was glad to close the Post Office door, its bell chiming, behind her.

The postmaster was a middle-aged gentleman with thinning brown hair and wore half moon glasses that had slipped halfway down his nose. He was serving a smartly dressed young woman. Laura immediately recognised her dress as one featured in the last edition of the *Ladies Home Journal*.

The postmaster was not to be hurried. He carefully weighed the young woman's parcel, using shiny brass weights on the scales, all the time keeping up a conversation about the state of the roads, the fallen trees and now the unseasonal heat. Laura browsed the display of sealing wax, string, brown parcel paper, pens and paper. No typewriter ribbons though.

'You're the newcomer up at Barton Court.'

She looked up to find herself being

scrutinised by a pair of pale green eyes. The young woman had finished her posting. She had a narrow face and thin lips, and porcelain skin. Auburn hair showed under her stylish hat, perched on one side of her head. She wore very expensive gold earrings set with green peridots.

'I am,' Laura agreed, moving to the counter and holding out her letter to her aunt. The postmaster gave her a kind smile, and put it on the scales. 'I'm Laura Crestwood.' She held out her hand and after a few seconds of hesitation the other woman allowed the tips of her gloved fingers to touch hers.

'What exactly are you doing up there?'

'I'm a secretary.'

'Goodness, how modern. Next thing we know we'll be getting telephones.' She turned her cool smile on the postmaster, letting her gaze slide over Laura's letter, which was address side up.

'That'll be sevenpence ha'penny,' the postmaster said. Laura passed him one of her last two shillings. He stamped her letter and then counted out the change. The young woman wasn't finished with her yet.

'And how do you find the mysterious Mr Colefax?'

'A considerate employer, so far, Miss -?'

'Beatrice Huntingdon. My family own Shute Priory. That's the big house on the edge of the village. We have a huge conservatory . . .'

35

'Indeed, possibly one of the biggest in the county,' came a teasing voice from the doorway. It was the man she'd seen talking to Brendan Colefax on her first morning. His clothes fitted immaculately and though he raised his hat politely, his blue eyes sparkled mischievously. 'And who have we here? Another newcomer to give the village gossips plenty to wag their tongues about. Colefax said he had some help arriving. He didn't say in such an attractive package.' He lifted her hand to his lips. The knowing look in his eyes told her he had seen her watching him. Laura felt herself flush as she introduced herself.

'You mustn't tease the poor girl, Edward,' Beatrice said, stepping forward and pushing her arm through his, her face suddenly alive.

'I expect Colefax is working you hard,' Edward said. 'Is there no end in sight to his mad experiments?'

'I've only just started and I don't really understand what he's doing, so I can't say when he'll be finished.'

'The sooner he takes all those poisonous things away the better,' Beatrice declared.

'I don't think he's going to be a permanent fixture on our doorstep,' Edward said, his eyes glittering. He held out his other arm. 'Care to join us, Miss Crestwood?'

She shook her head. 'Thank you, but I've other errands to do.' She indicated her basket.

'Of course. Another time. I'm Edward

Pascoe, by the way.' He tipped his hat. As he and Beatrice went into the street Laura thought she heard Beatrice say something about 'an adventuress'. Nothing further from the truth, Bea, she thought, I want nothing more than an obscure and quiet life.

The postmaster was right. It was getting hotter, Laura thought as she climbed the side lane from the butcher's shop, basket filled with purchases, including coffee. She'd been treated civilly, if not warmly welcomed. She had a sense that each shopkeeper wanted to hurry her along.

She paused for a moment outside the smithy. Despite the heat, a huge fire roared in the dark interior. The smithy roof was thatched, like many of the cottages in the village, and was open on two sides with stout wooden poles holding up the roof. The brick walls were hung with iron tools, horse shoes, and bellow. A small boy darted about fetching buckets of water from a full trough, while the smith held something in the fire. He was a big burly man with a stubble of black hair on his head and a wide leather belt under his bulging belly.

He swung the iron out of the fire onto the anvil and began to beat it. At the same time he began chanting in a loud voice, as if reciting from the Bible. 'And those that come from afar, bringing with them disease and pestilence, shall be scourged by the fire.'

37

Laura had been mesmerised by the sparks flying up from the mighty hammer, but now realised the words were directed at her. The smith knew she was there. Suddenly he looked directly at her, his eyes small and fierce. Without thinking she turned and heart racing walked away as fast as she could. After a few minutes she slowed down, annoyed with herself at taking flight like that. Had he really been threatening her?

She looked around, not recognising where she was. She was among older poorer cottages, well away from the central green. You imagined it, she chided herself. Why would the smith have wanted to threaten her?

'Are you lost, child?'

An elderly lady was standing in the open doorway of her cottage, wrinkled hands folded on top of a walking stick. She was dressed in black, with a not very clean apron over her dress. Her eyes were filmy.

'I am. I'm disoriented, and it's so hot.'

' 'tis unnatural. Come and sit here, maid, I'll fetch some lemonade.' She pointed to a wooden bench by her door, then fumbled her way inside. Laura sat down gratefully and put the basket at her feet.

The old lady returned with two glasses of lemonade on a tray and sat down beside her, feeling her way carefully. Could she be losing her sight, Laura wondered, going blind?

'You'm the young lass out at Barton Court,'

the old lady said. 'You've come a long way to our village. New people bring new ideas—and new trouble.'

Not this old lady too! 'I can assure you I don't bring any trouble with me. All I want is to earn my living and survive, like anyone else. Why am I so unwelcome here? Do people here think it's wrong for a woman to work?'

The old lady cackled with laughter. 'My, you've got some spirit! Plenty of women round here work hard all day. It's not that. It's what your Mr Colefax is up to.'

'He's a medical scientist and all he wants to do is help people.'

'That's as may be. All we know is that nothing's gone right since he arrived. First we had a drought, killing lots of young seedlings, then the storm washed what was left away, and now this heat. And I've heard that some animals are falling sick.'

'That's nothing to do with Brendan Colefax. He doesn't control the weather.' Laura drank her lemonade too fast and coughed as it caught the back of her throat.

'Maybe. But there's rumours of sick people being brought here. We don't need them. We've got enough sickness of our own. All those bangs and smells up there poisoning the soil, so they do say.'

'Well, "they" talk nonsense,' Laura declared firmly. 'I'm Laura by the way.'

'Gramma Neston, and I was born in this

cottage. Die in it too, no doubt. Last of the Nestons, that's me.'

'I'm sorry.'

'No need. There's a season for everything.'

A sudden thought occurred to Laura. This woman had lived in Manleigh all her life. She would know everyone roundabout.

'The night I arrived, in the storm, there was a girl. She was standing by the side of the road, alone and soaking wet. But when we went back to help her she'd vanished. Do you know if anyone is missing?'

Gramma Neston sat very still at her side, then nodded to herself. Laura thought she heard her whisper, 'So it's time then,' before going on more loudly, 'No one's missing. But it's going to get worse before it gets better.'

'If you say so, but I don't like to be that gloomy. Thank you for the lemonade. I'll need to be getting back now.'

Gramma Neston chuckled. 'That's it, you stand up for yourself. Wait a moment, I've got something for you.'

She pulled herself up on her stick and hobbled inside her cottage. Laura stood and tried to peer inside. There was a step down to a beaten earth floor, and just one chair and a table. Everywhere was festooned with bunches of drying flowers and grasses. On the table were a pestle and mortar and some small jars. A meagre fire burned in the grate with a big black stewpot over it.

40

'For you. Keep it under your pillow. It'll protect your sleep.' She placed a small bundle of herbs in Laura's hand. 'I must rest now. Come and see me again.'

'I will,' Laura promised.

As she walked slowly along the lane from Manleigh, the basket heavy on her arm, Laura examined the pot pourri Gramma Neston had given her. She was tempted to throw it away. But despite her enigmatic utterances, the old lady had been kind to her, and she liked her. It was likely she was the local herbalist and very knowledgeable.

Would Brendan Colefax have any faith in herbal remedies? Probably not. He would put his faith in chemicals and the laws of nature as proved by scientific experiment. The two were miles apart. No wonder the villagers were frightened. And where had that rumour of sick people arriving come from?

Laura couldn't help her thoughts turning to Edward Pascoe. He was very attractive, and Beatrice clearly thought so too. I hope I don't run in to her again, Laura thought. In fact that goes for Edward too. Too many complications. I must keep apart until I know I'm safe and forgotten, as I intend to forget them.

CHAPTER FOUR

'Laura—Miss Crestwood—I need your help. Urgently!'

Brendan Colefax thrust open the door to her office, barely pausing long enough to call out to her, before disappearing back into the laboratory. She stood up so quickly her chair fell to the floor and unquestioningly she ran after Brendan.

'Hold on to the end of this tube, above the receiving dish—yes, that's it . . .'

Heart still thumping, relieved he only wanted her to hold a piece of apparatus while he went to the other end of the bench, made some adjustments, then turned up the flame of the Bunsen burner. Liquid in glass flasks began to bubble, then flow, and then one by one droplets fell from the tube she held with one hand into the dish below. For a moment she'd thought he'd burned himself with acid from one of the big carboys that stood against the wall, or had set fire to his papers.

After some minutes of concentration he came to look into the dish, nodded with satisfaction, lifted the tubing slightly higher so the drops fell a little faster. She noticed that his fingers and the backs of his hands were stained with chemicals and scarred by small burns and cuts. He misinterpreted her intake of breath.

'Don't worry. There are no live bacilli—germs—anywhere in this room, whatever you might have heard to the contrary.' He gave a wry smile.

'The other day, when I went in to Manleigh, I did hear some rumours,' she said, glad of the chance to talk about it. Since she'd returned she'd barely seen him apart from at their evening meal, and she hadn't wanted to talk in front of Mrs Hannacott. Ever since seeing her deep in conversation with Tom, she hadn't been sure where the housekeeper's true loyalties lay. Brendan seemed to trust both her and Tom completely. Was it her own recent experience that made her question everyone's motives?

Their suppertime conversation had been confined to the weather, food, and Mrs Hannacott's extended family, a labyrinth of cousins, nephews and nieces, and great nephews and nieces. Her normally taciturn expression softened when she talked about the young children. She never mentioned a husband. She could either be a widow, or have assumed the 'Mrs' as housekeepers often did.

'Oh yes?' Brendan said, returning to the other end of the bench and turning off the burner. 'Tell you what, it's stifling in here. Why don't we close up for a bit and take a stroll in the fresh air.'

Laura went to straighten her desk and chair

43

and cover her typewriter while Brendan made everything safe and then washed his hands. They met at the door to the yard.

'If we go through that gate over there,' he pointed across the yard, 'We can follow the track across the field then turn off through the woods to a stream. It might be cooler there.'

It felt strange walking side by side with her employer as they followed the path across a meadow of waist-high drying grass rich with wild flowers and filled with the movement of butterflies and bees. He'd rolled back his sleeves, exposing strong sunburned arms. She could imagine her cousins sniffing with disapproval: not the act of a gentleman. Well, perhaps she didn't care for gentlemen after all.

'Is everything as you'd wish Miss Crestwood?' he asked.

'What? Oh you mean, my room and the office—I have everything I need. And Mrs Hannacott is a good cook.'

'I was lucky there. She was already installed, as part of the rental. I arrived on January the second and it was pouring with rain. I had to unload a cartful of delicate instruments. She went and fetched Tom, thank goodness, so it was soon done, and her hot soup afterwards seemed like the best thing I'd ever tasted!'

'You've been here nearly six months. Are you making any progress in your experiments?'

He swished at the long grass with his hand. 'Sometimes I think I am, and then there's a setback. It's very frustrating.' He looked at her. 'I suppose you must think it strange I don't tell you what I'm working on. That's partly so that when you type up the notes, you're not biased in any way, you just type exactly what I've written.'

'I barely understand anything of what I'm typing, so there's no chance of bias—more a danger I'll put the wrong symbol or word entirely,' she said with a laugh.

'Don't worry, I'll be checking everything over very carefully against my original. But you've had a broad education, more than some young women are blessed with.' He gave her an assessing glance.

'I have been very lucky,' she agreed. It was tempting to say more, to tell him about the betrayal she'd suffered and imagine his sympathetic response. But she could not risk revealing her secrets. 'You said partly just now. What's the other part?'

'Well.' He looked down consideringly and swished at the meadow grass again, sending up a cloud of bees and pollen. 'It goes back to the rumours you mentioned earlier. The less you know, the safer you are. I could be wrong of course.'

Wrong? Cousin Horace could never admit he was wrong. 'Safer? Is it really dangerous to work for you then? Am I about to get blown up?'

'I think you're teasing me,' he said with

mock severity. 'I shall make every effort not to blow anyone up. No, let's say I'm trying to find a cure for one of the deadliest diseases around. But it's backwards, I need to demonstrate that certain potions can't cure—the remedy lies in a completely different direction altogether. One that has been mocked but which I believe in, even if no one else does. Until I can prove it, though, I'm to be pilloried for it. Now you know the danger you're in. Society's disapproval.'

She thought of Aunt Rose and her own artist mother. 'I think I can bear that,' she said.

'Good. You're with me, then.' She saw the passion still gleaming in his eyes. 'It's the only way we can advance. If you'd seen some of the things I have, the poverty, the overcrowding, when just a few simple measures could help. But will the authorities listen? No. Remember how hard it was to persuade them that infected water caused cholera?'

'I wasn't alive then, but I've heard about it.'

He laughed. 'All right, I'm off my soap box now. Ah, here's the stile. Give me your hand and I'll help you over.'

His hand was firm and warm. She felt a tingle from his touch spread warmth through her body. She hoped he'd put her flushed appearance down to the heat. They turned off the main path now—that went on up the hill and eventually to Manleigh Village—and entered some woods in single file. After a

46

short distance they reached the riverbank.

'Not too many biting insects this time of day,' he said when they'd settled on the trunk of a fallen tree to watch the water trickling over its muddy bed. 'I've seen trout down here in the evening.'

'It's very peaceful.'

'When I was a lad on my father's estate I was allowed to roam and I used to build dams in the river and then swim in the pond I created.'

She heard a wistful note in his voice. 'Your father's estate?'

'Aye. It's a long way from here. We're— we're estranged.'

'My parents are dead,' she heard herself say. 'My father was an engineer and had been engaged on a project in Africa. They were sailing for Africa when a storm blew up. I still sometimes dream that they haven't really drowned but will turn up one day.'

'How old were you?'

'Nine. I was brought up by distant relatives.'

'That was the age I was when I started building dams.'

They were silent for a moment then Laura jumped up. 'I'd like to feel the water on my toes. If I go behind that bush there—'

'I'll walk upstream a little while you take your stockings off,' he assured her, understanding immediately.

It was a relief to peel off sticky stockings

and shoes, then walk to where the bank shelved down into a tiny beach. 'I'm ready,' she called.

Together they walked into the water, laughing as silt oozed up between their toes, examining the tiny fish and insects in the stream. For a few brief moments Laura felt all her cares roll away and she suddenly realised she felt lighthearted and happy.

Brendan offered her his handkerchief to dry her feet, and she rolled up her stockings and pushed them in her pocket, then they began to stroll back. I must remember he is still my employer, and call him Mr Colefax in front of Mrs Hannacott, she told herself, and pushed aside the tiny ache in her heart. This was just a moment of relaxation, nothing more. And anyway, she couldn't allow it to be more, not until she was twenty-one and free of the Middleships.

It was as they climbed back over the stile that she thought she saw a movement in the small copse on the top of the hill. A flash of a white face. Brendan was intent on jumping down.

'What is it?' he said, holding out his hand to her.

'Nothing—I just thought I saw someone watching us. Up on the hill. But there's nothing there now.'

Brendan shaded his eyes and stared at the copse. 'I can't see anything. Not that young girl again, do you think?'

'No. I thought it was a man. I must've been mistaken.'

It was Tom, she thought. I'm sure it was him. But if so, why didn't he call out to them? Had he been spying on them all along, or had he been to see Amy Hannacott and didn't want them to know? She knew Brendan trusted Tom, though.

She placed her hand in Brendan's once more, and jumped down, her shoes chafing her bare feet. Was it her imagination or did Brendan hold on to her hand a little longer than was strictly necessary? Well, if he had, she mustn't dwell on it. She was here only to work, to earn some money of her own, and decide her future. She must wait for Aunt Rose's reply—her aunt might ask her to come and live with her. She might even turn up in person!

As if able to read her thoughts Brendan began to discuss the next day's work. 'I've ordered some supplies from Bristol,' he told her. 'They're due on the train in three days' time. I'd like you to go and collect them.'

'Will I need to drive the cart?' she asked doubtfully.

'Mrs Hannacott or Tom will drive you,' he said. 'You'll need to sign for the goods, and oversee careful packing and—well, you'll see.'

'I'll see what?' she asked, curiosity piqued.

'Oh, nothing.' They'd reached the gate to the yard. 'I'm thirsty, are you? Let's go in and

49

get some tea.'

'Or lemonade. I hope there's some left—oh, what's that?' She pointed at the back door. 'Someone's left a bunch of—looks like weeds, stuck through the knocker.'

They'd arrived at the door now and Brendan reached out and took the bunch of wild plants which were tied together with a piece of twine. 'I hope this isn't meant to be a bouquet for Mrs Hannacott. It doesn't smell very nice.'

Laura sniffed and almost gagged. 'Ugh. Should we throw them away?'

Before he could answer the door swung open and Mrs Hannacott was staring out at them.

'Whatever for are you standing on the doorstep like that?' she chided. 'Come along in and—oh.' Her gaze fell on the plants in Brendan's hand 'Whatever's that?'

'They were lodged in the doorknocker. They've got a very pungent smell. Not ingredients you were expecting for supper I hope?'

Mrs Hannacott stepped closer, her ankle quite better now, and peered at the plants. 'Oh my goodness,' she said, going pale. 'That's a message that is. Henbane and—all sorts of poisonous plants. You be careful how you get rid of it. Good thing we don't have any livestock in the yard, kill them they would. Get rid of it carefully and wash your hands, you too

50

Miss Laura. You haven't touched your face have you? Some of they plants'll give you a rash.'

'I'll fetch some sacking from the laboratory,' Laura said. 'We can wrap them up.'

'Then Tom will know what to do with them,' Brendan agreed. 'But what do you mean, Mrs Hannacott, it's a message? Is someone trying to frighten you?'

'Not me, Master Colefax. The message is for you. Someone around here wants you gone. It's a warning—each plants spells something nasty, if you don't stop what you're doing and leave. It's a sort of magic spell, see.'

'What do you think Miss Crestwood?'

She saw weariness in his eyes. 'Nothing but superstition,' she declared. 'These plants can't harm us if we don't eat them. Bullies need to be stood up to and I've no intention of leaving.'

'What about you, Mrs Hannacott?'

'Oh, I'm all right.'

'We're agreed then, this message won't scare us off. Hurry up with that sacking Laura—Miss Crestwood.'

As Laura hurried to the laboratory all she could think of was seeing Tom on the hill. Had he really been there or was it just the breeze shifting the leaves on the trees? Only, if it had been him, it would explain why he'd wanted to hide. If he'd just been to Barton Court Farm and placed a sinister message on their door.

51

CHAPTER FIVE

Laura opened her eyes, woken as usual by the sound of birdsong and early morning sunshine filtering through the thin sprigged cotton curtain at her small window. She kept the little window open wide every night now to allow cool night air in. Each day seemed to be hotter than the one before. Despite the warm nights she was able to sleep, perhaps aided by the herbs Gramma Neston had given her, which she kept under her pillow. Or maybe she was just exhausted after hours of hard work each day.

Although she wanted to wriggle down under her sheet and blanket—she'd taken the eiderdown and other blankets off—as she would have done in London and waited for the maid to bring her tea and hot water to wash in, she made herself sit up. She picked up her mother's gold fob watch, which lay alongside her candlestick on the old wooden chair that served as her bedside table. It was seven o'clock. She finished the glass of water, also on her 'table', then got out of bed. She had time to write up her diary before washing and dressing.

She settled in the window seat after pulling aside the curtain, and wrote using a pencil, conserving her precious ink. 'Monday morning, start of my third week in Devon. Yesterday Brendan drove us into Bovey Tracey to attend church. I sponged down my check outfit. It was very hot. Mrs H said why didn't I wear a muslin dress and when I replied I only had two outfits Brendan overheard, and asked if I needed extra time to shop for summer dresses. I had to tell him I was waiting for my first wages. He was surprised and said why hadn't I asked for an advance! He said he was ordering me to go and buy more suitable summer clothes today, and would advance me half my month's wages. My first earnings!'

She paused and looked out of the window at the now familiar scenery, where the grass was fading from green to brown but the trees were still leafy. She was quite used to the quiet now.

Cousin Horace had never left her short of money, she thought. If she was absolutely truthful, she'd never felt neglected. She had new clothes, a comfortable life. It wasn't his or Venetia's fault that she'd felt as if she didn't fit in. They had their own four children, but had tried to be fair when childhood squabbles broke out.

She frowned. Which made it all the more hurtful. How could they plan to more or less *sell* her into a marriage? Had that been the only reason they'd looked after her all these years, as if fattening her up for market? She clenched her teeth in fury. She'd done the right thing, escaped when she could. She'd make her own way in the world, anything rather than marry a man forty years her senior. Mr Stillington. She felt sick at the thought of him. She'd been in his company only three or four times and she'd formed the impression of a cold and—and slimy man. She didn't like him at all, and on such a short acquaintance why had he chosen to offer for her hand? Surely Aunt Rose would agree?

Would there be a letter from her aunt yet? She counted the days, how long her letter would've taken to reach Turkey, how long for a reply to come back. Depending on whether her aunt was near civilisation, and replied straight away. Maybe Aunt Rose would send a telegraph instead. She'd put the Post Office address as well as Barton Court Farm.

Quickly she scribbled: 'Today I go into the village to buy a new dress and to check at the Post Office for a telegraph.' Then she closed her diary, poured water from the jug she'd brought up the night before into the bowl to wash. Cold water was just right in this heat. She'd seen Brendan put his head under the pump in the yard to cool off. Her heart quickened at the image of him, droplets of water in his hair, wet shirt clinging to him. He'd been unaware that she was observing him, and his face wore that thoughtful serious look that was becoming habitual with him.

He'd left them after church yesterday and gone off on an errand of his own, without saying where. She'd heard him come back after midnight stumbling in the dark in the yard. In fact, she hadn't been able to get to sleep till she'd heard him return safely.

'Foolish Laura,' she said softly to herself, and tried to pretend it was only because she and Mrs Hannacott needed his protection.

When she entered the kitchen she saw a place only laid for one at the table. 'Good morning, Mrs Hannacott,' she said. 'Has Mr Colefax had breakfast already?'

'He said for some of this 'ere coffee to be taken over to the 'boratory. I'll pour yours first, then take the rest over and I've put bread and butter and cheese on and all, whether he likes it or not. You've fried eggs in the pan there.' She poured Laura a cup.

'That's a handsome silver coffeepot,' Laura said. Previously Mrs Hannacott had been using an old saucepan.

'Mr Colefax give it to me this morning. He must've got it last night and no, I don't know where he went.' Mrs Hannacott gave her a knowing look.

'Oh.' Laura poured a little cream into her coffee, while Mrs Hannacott prepared the tray for Brendan. She noticed her adding a posy of sweet peas. 'Those are pretty,' she said.

'Tom brung them over this morning with the eggs and milk. I've put the rest by for the table. You're off into Manleigh this morning,' she went on briskly. 'I've made a list for you, it's in

55

the basket. Just make sure you give the smithy a wide berth. That Jed Parr can't stop his tongue from wagging.'

I wonder who gave Brendan that silver coffeepot, Laura thought as she dished up her eggs. And why did Tom bring Mrs Hannacott flowers? To make up for putting those weeds on the door?

The air was hot and heavy in the deep country lane. Flies buzzed in the still air. She took off her bonnet to try and keep cool. Unseasonal, unnatural. She'd heard those words so many times yesterday as everyone complained about the heat. In the pew behind her two farmers discussed opening up old wells and resorting to stored water, and how they feared for the wheat in the fields. But at least in a larger town like Bovey, she and Brendan were not singled out for attack.

I'll visit Gramma Neston again, she thought. I think I've persuaded her that Brendan's work is no threat to the village. But first, would there be any message from her Aunt?

The post master shook his head. 'Sorry Miss Crestwood. Nothing for you today,' as he took the letters Brendan had left out for her to mail to his suppliers. Disappointed, she made her way down a side street to the haberdashery and drapers store. She hoped she could afford not only one of the new ready made dresses, but also material and one of the new patterns. She would make a dress for herself. All those

56

sewing lessons the Middleships insisted she have would now come in useful.

As she reached out for the handle, the door opened with a ping of the bell, and Beatrice Huntingdon blocked her way. She wore a well fitting white dress, carried a parasol and a brown paper parcel in her white gloved hands. Laura immediately felt drab and stained.

'Why, it's Mr Colefax's *secretary*,' she said, not offering her hand to shake. 'Need some mending materials perhaps? I've just had a fitting for a new dress. It was featured in this month's *Ladies Home Journal* and Miss Duckett is going to copy it. I don't expect you've seen it.'

'The one with the detail on the hem?' Laura couldn't resist answering, then wished she hadn't. Was she giving too much away?

Beatrice's pale green eyes flashed. 'You've read it then. And when are you going back to wherever you've come from to visit your family?'

Laura hesitated. No, she mustn't give anything away. 'My aunt will be visiting soon,' she said shortly. 'Good day Miss Huntingdon.' And she pushed past her into the shop.

*   *   *

'. . . And this is the material I'm going to make up myself.' She pulled open the corner of the parcel. 'It's pale blue cotton.' She held it out

57

for Gramma Neston to feel, aware that the old lady probably couldn't see the colour in the bright sunlight. The old lady's claw-like hands fingered the fabric her faded eyes could barely see.

'You'll look proper handsome in that, maid. You want to wear it to the Village Fair. Now, what's that young man of yours been up to?' She suddenly peered sharply at Laura.

'My young—oh, you mean Br—Mr Colefax. Nothing, beyond continuing with his work.'

Gramma Neston shook her head. 'There's something else going on. Something I can't see—for one thing, this heat, it's—'

'Unnatural! I know, I know. People round here seem to think it's Mr Colefax's fault. How could he have conjured up a heatwave, it's a natural phenomenon!'

Gramma laughed. 'My, such long words. You'll make my head spin. But I was going to say, this heat is bad for the farmers, and as that's how folk round here survive, growing food and rearing animals, you and your young man will have your parts to play. That's all I'm saying.'

'I'm sorry Gramma. I should've known you'd understand.'

'I understand more than most. Some say it's a gift, but sometimes it's a curse.' She grasped Laura's hand suddenly, her grip surprisingly strong. 'Have you seen her again?'

'Who?'

'The lost child, of course.'

'No. Why, do you know who it is now?'

Gramma muttered something Laura could not understand, then said more clearly, 'No, I can't say as I do. I must go and rest now.'

Laura saw that she was looking tired. She took a small packet from her pocket. 'Here's some tea—to thank you for my lemonade.'

'Thank you, child. Remember, I'll be watching over you.'

As she walked slowly uphill towards the village centre, keeping in the shade as much as she could, Laura puzzled over whether she'd heard Gramma correctly. Did she say 'over you' or 'out for you'?

'There she is. She's the one we should be getting answers from?'

Too late, Laura realised she was in front of the smithy. She'd been so lost in her thoughts she'd forgotten to go the long way round. Jed Parr the blacksmith, all six feet of him with broad shoulders and protected by a leather apron today, pointed an accusing finger at her.

'What—what do you mean?' She kept the tremble of fear from her voice.

Three men blocked her way past the smithy. They wore working clothes, gaiters and boots, their heads covered by drooping felt hats. They all obeyed Jed and stared at her.

'Animals is dying now, see,' one of them ventured, though not as accusingly as Jed. 'Two of my pigs, dead in the sty this morning.'

59

'And Zekiel's sheep—don't forget the sick sheep,' Jed thundered, glowering at her.

Another man nodded, shrugging his shoulders helplessly. 'Don't know what's wrong with them. Never seen the like before. Coming along lovely they were, and now . . .' He shrugged again.

'I know why. It's Colefax. Poisonous fumes from his chemicals and who knows what else, killing our animals. We don't want him here,' Jed thundered.

Laura lifted her chin. 'If there were any poisonous gases then Mrs Hannacott, me and old Champion would be affected, let alone Mr Colefax. But we're all perfectly all right. Mr Colefax wants to help people—'

'That's just it. He helps his own, and sends all the poisons our way. You tell him to take his chemicals and all his sick people somewhere else.'

'Contamination, that's what it is,' the third man contributed, beetling his bushy grey brows.

'We don't know for sure,' the first man said.

'Rubbish, Andrew. You've got two dead pigs that says—'

'Then I challenge you,' Laura said. 'You bring your dead animal to Mr Colefax for investigation.'

'That pig goes nowhere,' the smith thundered. 'He'll only lie about what he finds out.'

Laura bristled, about to defend Brendan's honour, when a voice cut in from behind her. 'That's enough. You've had your fun, now leave her alone.'

'We're only speaking the truth, Master Pascoe.'

'I understand your concerns, Jed. This is my village too. How about I have a word with Colefax and report back? Come, Miss Crestwood, take my arm.' He lifted his hat.

She took his arm and they walked across the green, she sure they were still being stared at.

'They don't mean any harm,' Edward told her. 'They're just worried about their livelihood.'

'I understand but Jed is—intimidating.'

'True. He always wins our local strong man competition at the Village Fete. It's taking place soon, you can see him in action for yourself. You must come, there'll be dancing afterwards. Can you dance, Miss Crestwood?'

She smiled. 'I can.'

'Then I shall claim the first dance with you. Now, give me your basket and package. I shall give you a lift to Barton Court, I've got the gig here today.'

'Oh, that isn't necessary—'

'It will be my pleasure. Then I can have a word with Colefax and clear up this misunderstanding right away.' He grinned wickedly at her. 'Got to pretend to play my part as the local landowner's son, you know.

Here we are.' He placed her basket and package on the floor of the gig. A well groomed chestnut pony stood between the shafts. She stroked its velvety nose and it whickered.

'This is Pickles,' he said. 'Everyone loves Pickles.' He patted the pony's neck then handed her up before jumping lightly aboard himself. As they trotted away Laura had the uneasy feeling that Beatrice might be watching them, eyes like chips of green ice.

'Since I saw you last I've been up to London to visit my sister and her brood,' Edward said and, as Pickles picked his way along the lanes, Edward took her briskly through the dances, soirees, theatre and music he'd enjoyed while up there. She also gleaned some knowledge of the progress of fledgling romances among acquaintances they both knew, but she gave nothing away, pretending a polite interest.

'My other sister's married too, lives near Bristol. Then there're my two young brothers, both away at school. Feller gets a bit bored stuck away down here. Do you get a bit bored?' he looked at her flirtatiously and leaned a little closer.

She took his question seriously and thought for a moment. She remembered being bored in stuffy drawing rooms exchanging tittle tattle over endless cups of tea in the company of Cousin Venetia, or sitting in draughty halls listening to even more endless lectures on improving oneself, or simply sewing some pointless piece of embroidery through long evenings while Cousin Horace read aloud from approved texts or played on the harmonium.

'No, I can honestly say I've never felt so unbored in my life,' she told him.

Edward responded with a grin. 'Then I shall take that as a compliment. Perhaps things are looking up in Manleigh.'

Before she could reply they swung into the yard and Edward pulled up the gig outside the laboratory. Brendan came to the door and watched as Edward helped her down. He acknowledged Edward with a nod then said to Laura, 'I'm glad you're back. I need your help with mixing some solutions.'

'I'll put everything away and come right over,' Laura said.

'Aren't you going to thank me for rescuing Miss Crestwood and bringing her back to you in one piece, then? And a glass of something cold wouldn't go amiss.'

Brendan's face darkened as he looked from Edward to Laura and back. 'What's been going on?'

'Few of the villagers gave her a message to pass on to you.'

'Is this true? Have they been harassing you again Laura? I'm beginning to think you shouldn't go into the village any more. Certainly not on your own.'

63

'Honestly, I'm all right. It was my fault. Mrs Hannacott warned me to avoid the smithy. It was Jed again, and three farmers. Two animals have died, some others are sick, and they're blaming you—or rather, your chemicals. I told them it was nonsense but—'

'Luckily I came along and whisked her away, and I said I'd take a look myself. So why don't you show me around while Laura fetches me that drink.'

Brendan hesitated then stood aside. 'Feel free but don't touch anything. Laura, ask Mrs Hannacott for a glass of cider for Mr Pascoe.'

'If I survive, that is!' Edward said with a laugh and wink to her.

Mrs Hannacott must have heard them talking, because she was already pouring cider from a demijohn into a jug. Silently Laura went to wash her hands then fetched two glasses and a tray. Mrs Hannacott filled the glasses and they looked at one another, still in silence, then Laura went outside. She could hear raised voices from inside the laboratory. Had Edward knocked something over and ruined an experiment?

Then Edward stormed out, saying, 'I'll be d—d if I do!' He took one of the glasses Laura held out, drained it down in one go, then leapt into the gig.

'You heed my words, I don't speak lightly,' Brendan called out as Edward geed Pickles into a fast trot.

'What happened? He doesn't believe us?' Laura asked dismayed as they watched the gig disappear down the drive.

'What? Oh, I don't know and frankly I don't care what he thinks.'

'So what were you arguing about?'

He wouldn't meet her eyes. 'Something else entirely. The rent. He wants to put the rent up.'

Laura wasn't convinced. 'Edward Pascoe is our—your landlord?'

'His father is. I doubt he knows what his son is getting up to.' He turned and went back into the laboratory, leaving Laura with the distinct impression the two men had been arguing about something quite different.

CHAPTER SIX

'A dead pig has mysteriously appeared by the yard gate,' Brendan said coming into the kitchen the next morning as Laura sat at breakfast. 'Did it make its own way here before it died, or is it another message from the village, do you think, Mrs Hannacott?'

'A pig? No, can't think of any meaning to that.'

'Er—I think it's because of me,' Laura said.

Both Brendan and Mrs Hannacott looked at her with curiosity.

'When I was in the village yesterday I gave them a challenge, I'm afraid. I said that if they gave you one of the animals that was sick, or had died, you would be able to find out what had happened to it. I didn't think anyone would take me up on it.'

'It's human physiology I know about, rather than animals,' Brendan said doubtfully.

'Jed told them that they couldn't trust your findings anyway. You'd just make up whatever you wanted. Even if I was writing up the results.'

'Jed's not a very trusting sort of man, is he. But someone in the village clearly trusts you, even if I'm still open to question,' Brendan said slowly, rubbing his chin. He sat down at the table. 'Mrs Hannacott, another pot of coffee please. Laura, I want to hear every detail of what took place yesterday in the village, every scrap of information you have, every word you overheard. And then we'll get that poor dead carcass into a safe place.'

'I'm sorry if I put you in a difficult position,' Laura said as Mrs Hannacott busied herself at the range. 'Their accusations made me angry, and I said the first thing that came into my head.' Then, feeling herself flush, she added hastily, 'Because they were so ill-informed.'

'They've not had your advantages,' Mrs Hannacott observed, putting the coffee pot down on the table. 'But doesn't excuse their behaviour to you, now, does it. I've known those men all my life, and I've never known them like this before. Live and let live, that's what folks around here are usually like. Everything's changed. I blame the railways. Next thing it'll be these fangled telephones.'

'Thank you Mrs Hannacott.' Brendan looked at her thoughtfully. 'It's helpful to know that this isn't their usual attitude. As you said earlier, they're driven by fear, but then they must have faced disasters before, bad weather, failed harvests. Something is different this time. Amy—Mrs Hannacott—could you get hold of Tom for us, to help move the animal?'

Laura held her own counsel. Something was niggling at the back of her mind. Yes, the farmers were facing a difficult time and were concerned for their crops and animals, but something else was stirring in the village, as Brendan had just said. She didn't agree with Mrs Hannacott that it was the arrival of modern inventions. The farmers used all sorts of new machinery that made their life easier and improved their yields. No, there was something else behind it. And her money was on Tom. Brendan obviously trusted Tom. Mrs Hannacott was very friendly with him too— though that made her unsure of where the housekeeper's loyalties really lay. Something didn't add up. But until she was sure of her ground, it was best to say nothing.

'Now then Laura,' Brendan brought her

back to the present by pouring coffee and offering her cream and sugar. 'Don't hold back anything of your visit to Manleigh yesterday.' He brought out the pad and pencil he used for jotting down thoughts. 'In science we must examine every fact coolly and rationally. I hope I've taught you that much already.'

Once he had written it down, even her encounters with Beatrice and Gramma Neston, he stared at the page for a long time, lost in his own thoughts and forgetting Laura and his cooling coffee.

'Do you think you might be able to discover the illness these poor animals have contracted?' she asked cautiously.

'What? Oh yes, I'm quite confident about that. I shall take some samples and send them off to one of my university friends who went into animal science. He's at Cambridge now. The problem will be, how to get Jed and the others to accept his findings, whatever they might be.' He suddenly smiled at her. Her heart gave a sudden leap and sped up. 'Thanks for believing in me, Laura. It means a great deal to me. Especially after—well, no need to go into that.'

If Mrs Hannacott hadn't come bustling in through the back door, Laura was sure he would have taken her hand.

'I caught up with Andrew's lad. Working in the top field he is, and he'll get a message to Tom. Oh, that's a bit of a climb,' she fanned herself and sat down at the table with them.

'Excellent. Now Laura, I've got a mission for you. Once Tom's helped me, then he'll take you in to Hamholt Station.'

'More supplies?'

'Just a few items—but there's something for you too.' His eyes gleamed suddenly. She glimpsed the young carefree man underneath the serious and driven medical scientist.

'What is it?' Laura's throat constricted with anxiety. He hadn't been contacted by her second cousins and, misguidedly, thinking it was for her benefit, invited them to Devon?

'You'll see. It's for my benefit as well, I should say—and Mrs Hannacott's.'

The housekeeper had been following their exchange closely. Now she made a humphing noise and stood up. 'I need to get on, or we won't have any lunch today,' and made her way into the scullery.

Brendan stood up too, then turned back. 'You're wearing the new dress you bought yesterday, aren't you.'

'You noticed! I am, and it's so much cooler.'

'My sister has trained me to notice such things. That creamy colour suits you.' She felt colour rise in her cheeks, and he hastily added, 'I was just thinking, you'll need to protect it. Not very practical for our work.'

When he'd gone, she sat for a moment. He'd paid her a compliment and then, as her employer, thought better of it. Of course, he wouldn't want to mislead her. Unlike Edward Pascoe, who clearly thought she would be taken in by his flirtatious manner. Of the two men, Edward was the more classically handsome. And he was very well off. But she wasn't drawn to him in the same way as she was drawn to Brendan. Working alongside him each day, the hours flew by, and she knew she was in danger of finding what true happiness felt like. A danger because at some point she would have to leave, and that would be very painful.

Surely it was only that she was lonely and vulnerable, so far away from the people and places she knew and his was a sympathetic face. That was all. That would *have* to be all.

It seemed only a short while till Tom arrived and with little fuss the carcass was removed to an old outbuilding so that Brendan could begin his work. Laura glanced out of her office window to see if he was ready to take her to Hamholt. The trap was indeed ready, with Champion, looking very unkempt after the Pascoes' Pickles, harnessed up. But Tom was instead heading for the back door to the farmhouse.

As Laura watched, the door opened. Had Mrs Hannacott been waiting for him to come over to her? Heads close together they talked earnestly for a few minutes. Normally Tom barely spoke more than two words together, and certainly not to her. But with Amy

Hannacott he became quite animated, his hands waving about as he explained something. He then took something out of his pocket and gave it to Mrs Hannacott, who stood on tiptoe and kissed his cheek before going inside again.

Amy Hannacott kissing Tom—what was his surname? He was only ever referred to as Tom—on the cheek. What was that about? Was he too one of her tribe of relatives who seemed to fill the neighbourhood?

I'm not looking forward to being in the same cart as him for half an hour, she thought. Perhaps I can sit in the back and I won't worry about having to try to talk to him? Though if I do sit beside him, maybe I can prise some information out of him?

In the end, it was her choice where she sat. Tom heaved himself stiffly into the driver's seat, leaving her to clamber up as best she could, making sure not to catch her new pale yellow dress on anything rusty or oily. She plonked herself down beside him and smiled brightly. It was impossible to tell from his expression if he was pleased or annoyed.

They set off at a steady trot, all of Tom's concentration on the horse and the road ahead. She noticed that his hands were brown and calloused, and the tip was missing from the little finger of his left hand.

'Those are lovely eggs you've been bringing Mrs Hannacott,' she tried after a while.

'Hens are laying well,' he replied then lapsed into silence again.

How could she find out where he stood with the other villagers, particularly Jed the blacksmith?

'Do you live in Manleigh Village itself, or on one of the farms?' she enquired.

He cast her a glance from the corner of his eyes as if he guessed what she was up to. 'I does.'

'Actually in the village? Do you know Gramma Neston?'

'Everyone knows Gramma. 'Twas her herbs saved my hand from going septic when it got caught in the sawing machine.' He waggled the maimed little finger at her.

'She's very wise. And you live near her?'

'Not far,' came the unhelpful reply.

She tried another tack. 'It's very sad what's happening to the animals. Do you think that pig was one of Farmer Andrew's?'

'You'd best ask him,' was all he would say.

'It's not Mr Colefax's fault. And I know he's going to be able to prove it.'

He was silent for a moment, then said, 'There are some cattle sick today too. They do say this heat is—'

'—unnatural. Yes, I know,' she finished for him. 'What's wrong with the cows?'

He shook his head. 'No idea.'

He wasn't going to reveal his private opinions, and she suspected that he wouldn't even if she asked him a direct question. And if she did that, she would be revealing too much of her suspicions. She needed real answers to her questions.

After a while she said, 'Will you be showing your hens at the village fête?'

For some reason he found this funny. His shoulders shook, as he struggled to say, 'No, not the hens. Egg's'll be for sale, though.'

'Edward—Mr Pascoe—was telling me about the fête. He said I should come, and have a dance.'

He turned and looked at her properly for the first time. 'You're going to the dance with young Pascoe?'

Was that disapproval? Recklessly she said, 'I expect I shall dance with him, yes. Will you be dancing?'

'Everyone will be there,' he said, and then rode the rest of the way in silence.

'Morning Tom, morning Miss Crestwood.' The stationmaster heard them clatter into Station Approach and came out to greet them. 'Train was on time, your goods are here.' He smiled up at Laura. 'Better weather than the day you arrived, eh.'

'Yes.' She managed to smile back, though she felt her heart begin to race with anxiety again. Somehow the station seemed linked to London, almost as if the rails had the power to drag her back to her old life.

'Look over here,' he went on. 'Those are the

73

goods for Mr Colefax.' He pointed at a couple of wicker baskets. These, she knew, would be lined with straw to protect their contents. 'And that must be yours.' He pointed again. She looked in the direction he was pointing and then gasped in surprise. A bicycle was leaning against the wall.

'The cycle do you mean?' she asked, thinking, no, I must be making a mistake.

'Yes. Came this morning, for Mr Colefax. Only it's a lady's bicycle, and I don't think it's for Amy Hannacott somehow.'

She walked over and took hold of the handlebars, testing its weight. Not too heavy. She looked at the name of the manufacturer, emblazoned in red letters. A good maker. There was a solid basket attached in front of the handlebars.

Would she remember how to ride it? Conscious that Tom and the stationmaster were watching her closely, she wheeled it out into the forecourt and stepped into position. Then it was up into the saddle and reaching for the pedals. After a few false starts, she safely rode it round the yard. The stationmaster clapped delightedly. 'Well done, Miss,' he said.

So this was the surprise Brendan had said would be waiting for her. As he'd also said, it would make journeying to the shops much easier, once she'd learned how to cope with the hills. She imagined Jed's face as she rode into the village! He'd probably think it was the instrument of the devil.

'It's wonderful,' she said. 'I'll ride it back to Barton Court Farm after I've helped you load up, Tom.'

'I've never seen the like,' was his grudging reply.

*   *   *

Had there been this many hills on the way to the village before, Laura wondered as she wheeled the bicycle up a particularly steep rise. Fortunately there was a long dip down afterwards, and then it was relatively flat if she cut through and joined the main road from Hamholt, through the woods to the long driveway.

Her legs ached from unaccustomed pedalling, and her arms ached from pushing the bike, but she didn't mind. This machine spelled freedom. Had Brendan been thinking of her own needs as well as his own when he ordered it? The thought warmed her.

At last she was at the top, mounted again and freewheeled down the long slope, hand on the steadying brakes. The basket on the front contained several packets wrapped in brown paper. There were new wicks for the oil lamps. Mrs Hannacott had spent quite a bit of time restoring and polishing the rusted lamps dotted throughout the house, which would give

75

them much more light in the evening than candles. There were some brass clamps and nuts and bolts for Brendan from the hardware store. And also some worsted stockings for Mrs Hannacott. How could she bear to wear them in this continuing heat? Perhaps she'd heard about the sale at 'The Changing Rooms' dress and fabric emporium, and was putting them by for the winter.

Laura gripped the handlebars tighter as she remembered what happened as she left the dress shop, clutching not only Mrs Hannacott's parcel but the blue cotton dress which she'd decided to have made up after all rather than sew it herself. She had the misfortune to bump into Beatrice and a friend of hers, walking arm in arm towards her. She gave a cursory nod and grabbed hold of the bicycle, hoping to escape. She heard Beatrice say something in a low voice to her friend and they both giggled. But then she called out, 'How very strange. Do tell, are you being forced to mount that machine by your employer, or do you actually enjoy it.'

'I enjoy it,' she replied shortly, wheeling it into the road and testing the brakes and glancing at the tyres. She wouldn't put it past Jed to send a boy to let her tyres down.

'Very unladylike,' her friend said. 'You must think you're a man.'

They laughed again. Laura ignored them and swung her leg over, ready to mount up.

They pretended to be shocked and covered their eyes, laughing some more.

'Tell you what, you should give rides on that at the village fête. But I don't expect you'll be allowed to come.'

Laura couldn't help herself. 'Oh yes, I shall be there. Mr Pascoe says he'd like to dance with me.'

Beatrice's eyes flashed angrily. 'Poor Edward,' she managed. 'As the squire's son he has to dance with just anybody.' And she swept her friend on by. I wonder if she saw I was in the village and came out deliberately to bump into me and bait me, Laura wondered.

She smiled to herself now as she cycled slowly through the woods, unconsciously glancing from side to side, in case she saw that lost child again. It had been a cheap shot but she wasn't going to let Beatrice get the better of her.

She rang the bike's bell as she rode into the yard and Brendan came to the laboratory door.

'How was your ride?' he asked. 'Is it a good machine?'

'It's perfect,' she said, and couldn't help grinning. 'It handles really well. I'll have to get a repair and maintenance kit. The hardware store said they can order one for us.' She handed him his packet of goods.

'I'd like to try and ride it myself, even if it is a lady's bike. Shall we have a lesson after supper?'

'Of course! Though you'll be sore if you fall off in this yard.'

'I shall have to make sure not to fall off,' he said solemnly. 'No trouble in the village today? I really don't like the thought of you going there alone now.'

She shook her head. 'As long as I steer clear of Jed there's no problem. Apart from a couple of young women laughing at me. They said I should show the bicycle at the fête, hire it for rides.'

'You'd like to go the fête, wouldn't you,' he said slowly.

'I think I would. And Edward Pascoe said there will be dancing in the evening.'

'Hmm. I expect he'll want to dance with you.'

'Oh, that. Well, as Beatrice said, he has to dance with everyone, as the squire's son. Will you come?'

He rubbed his chin thoughtfully, a gesture she was beginning to find very familiar. 'Might be a good idea. Give me a chance to do some more delving for answers and information.'

'And will you stay for the dancing too? Can you dance?'

'A clumsy scientist like me?' His eyes gleamed. 'You'll have to wait and see.'

CHAPTER SEVEN

Fingers slippery with perspiration, Laura put the final stitch in place, tied off, then held the straw hat up for inspection before trying it on in front of the mirror. Mrs Hannacott had told her about the 'Best Bonnet' competition at the Fair, and so she'd made flowers out of scraps of material and had now sewn them on to a straw hat.

'It looks home-made, and very badly,' she told her reflection in the tiny mirror.

It didn't resemble the design she'd had in her mind's eye. The 'flowers' all flopped and it looked a bit of a mess, she thought. But even if she came last, at least she'd tried.

She'd chosen to wear the new blue cotton dress. It fitted her very well and she still couldn't believe how reasonable the local seamstress's price had been. She'd have paid three times that much in London. She looked in the mirror again. The dress was lovely, but the hat was a disaster!

Even though Mrs Hannacott still kept a wary distance, Laura thought as she ran downstairs, surely she would not let Laura make a complete fool of herself.

Inside the kitchen she skidded to a halt. Brendan sat at the kitchen table, with a cup of coffee and a newspaper laid out before him.

She glanced at the mantel clock. Yes, it said ten o'clock. But he wasn't in his laboratory.

'Hello, Laura,' he said. 'It's going to be a good day for the Fair. I'm told it usually rains on Manleigh Village Fair, but not today it seems.'

She nodded, feeling her hat wobble. 'Six weeks without rain. I'm beginning to believe what they say, that it is unnatural.'

He looked at her hat. 'That's very pretty. Is it for today?'

She groaned. 'I made it. I wanted to ask Mrs Hannacott if it was too ridiculous to wear.'

'It's not ridiculous. You've obviously gone to a lot of effort.' She tried to work out if he was being polite, or really meant what he was saying. 'But I can see from the look on your face that you can't take the word of a mere man.'

'Your sister has taught you very well!'

'Mrs Hannacott is in the pantry, checking on her home-made produce. Why don't you ask her opinion?'

'Someone taking my name in vain? I was just—oh!' Mrs Hannacott, carrying a basket of jars of jam and jelly, stopped short at the sight of Laura's hat.

'I thought so, it's terrible. Never mind, I don't have to enter for any of the competitions.'

'No, it's very good. You just need to get some of those blooms more upright. I've got just the thing, some wire. Give it to me.' She put the basket on the table, took the hat and disappeared back into the pantry.

Laura sat down at the table. 'I'll make up for any missed time next week,' she told Brendan. 'You're sure you don't mind me taking the day off today?'

'I don't, and in fact I've decided to come to the Fair too. Tom's going to take us in the trap. Do you want to put your bicycle in the back?'

'Yes, please.' Laura's pulse began to race with delight at the thought that Brendan was coming too. Not that he'd want to spend the day in her company. He'd have his own things to do, but he'd be there—and perhaps he might dance with her?

'Does that mean you've discovered why the animals are dying?' In the past weeks the mysterious death toll had mounted, affecting cattle, sheep and pigs. There were no signs of any of the usual infections, such as foot and mouth. It was random and inexplicable.

'I've got a theory,' Brendan said, leaning his elbows on the table, as he did when he got enthusiastic about something. 'But it's a very wild one. I'm hoping to learn more today at the Fair.'

Laura hid the stab of disappointment. Of course he wasn't coming because of her. And that was for the best. She knew that, over the weeks they'd built an easy camaraderie, that was all. They worked well together, it didn't and wouldn't go further.

'Here you are,' Mrs Hannacott bustled in again.

'That looks so much better. Thank you!' Laura admired the hat, its false blooms now perky and more real. 'It's not a winner but perhaps I won't come last.'

'Best get on your way.' Mrs Hannacott said, her guard back up again. 'I'll make my own way later when I've got my contributions sorted out.' She indicated the basket.

'I didn't realise how big it would be,' Laura said to Brendan when they arrived.

Manleigh Summer Fair was laid out in two fields close to the village. Under the cloudless blue sky sprawled a profusion of tents, stalls, animal pens, and machinery.

He nodded. 'There'll be farmers and workers from a wide area here today, not just Manleigh. I want to look at the livestock. I suggest we meet again at the refreshment tent about 5 o'clock.'

Laura felt a twinge of concern as she watched him disappear into the throngs around the stalls. What if he encountered Jed Parr the blacksmith? But he had seemed unconcerned, eager even, to follow up his investigations. She already knew him well enough to know that once his mind was focussed, nothing could sway him.

She enjoyed wandering among the stalls,

making some purchases, greeting the few villagers who recognised her. She was pleased to find a good queue of women and children lined up to have a ride on her bicycle at the allotted hour, their payments to be donated to the poor fund. She glimpsed Beatrice Huntingdon, looking cool under her chic parasol while she was getting pinker and hotter out in the sun as she instructed her audience in the intricacies of the bicycle, but she didn't care. She'd rather be involved than a bystander.

Finally just before the Refreshment Tent opened, it was time for the Best Bonnet competition. She hurried along, trying to rub bike oil from her hands, and arrived just in time to take her stand in the line—only to find to her disquiet that Beatrice was right at the front of the crowd of spectators. The judges were the vicar and his wife. To her surprise she came third. The winner was a young village mother whose beautiful hat was covered in wild flowers.

'First prize goes to Polly, and will be awarded by its donor, Miss Huntingdon.'

Laura watched as Beatrice gave Polly a pair of kid gloves. What use she would she have for those? Apart from selling them to make much needed cash to feed her children, Laura thought.

'Never mind,' Beatrice said, brushing by her, 'At least you look like one of the village now.

It's one way to try and get them to accept you, I suppose. But they never will.'

Laura stared at her, willing her mind to come up with something clever in response, when she heard Brendan's quiet words at her shoulder.

'Third prize, well done Laura.'

Laura's heart skipped a beat at the sound of his voice, as Beatrice lifted her chin, smirked, pretended not to see him, and went on her way.

'Shall we go and get our place in the Refreshment Tent?' Brendan suggested, ignoring Beatrice's rudeness.

Laura nodded, not trusting herself to speak. She smarted on his behalf at the way people in Manleigh were treating him, but sensed he would rather not talk about it. She fell into step beside him, taking off the flowery bonnet and teasing out her hair, hoping it hadn't gone too flat from the heat and her perspiration. He'd taken off his necktie and undone his shirt, his skin lightly tanned.

'I've seen some amazing machinery this morning,' he was telling her, as he eased their passage through the crowds, seemingly oblivious to the occasional muttered remark or angry stare directed at him. 'There's a plough operated by two steam engines either side of a field that pull it first one way then back again. And there are developments in threshing machinery too . . .' As she listened to his enthusiastic description of all he had seen she regained control over her emotions.

They collected food and then, sitting at one of the long trestle tables in the tent—strangers from further afield sat next to them—she became so engrossed in their conversation that she was able to forget the animosity of the Manleigh villagers. By the time they had finished eating the fiddlers were tuning up and space was being cleared for dancing to begin. The sunlight was slanting in the sky but the day's heat still hung heavy in the air. Even her new cotton dress was sticking to her.

'Did you learn anything more about animals falling sick?' she finally asked him.

He grimaced. 'At one point the blacksmith, Jed, confronted me. He told me that more cattle and sheep had been found sick, and there have been some more deaths. He asked me when I was going to stop my unholy practices, and when I told him I was not going anywhere, he swore at me that he'd find a way to get rid of me.'

Laura shook her head. 'Jed can be frightening when he starts shouting, but it's all bluster isn't it?'

Brendan's mouth set in a firm line. 'I'm not going to let the Jeds of this world undermine the important work I'm doing. You're right, so far it's been a war of words. Let's hope it stays that way.'

'If only you'd got the investigation into the

pig completed, then you'd have been able to put him right.'

'There are still some loose ends to be tied up there,' he answered evasively. 'I'm still waiting on some information as well as the results from my friend in Cambridge.'

'I can't wait to see the look on his face and the other villagers too, when you are able to clear your name,' she blurted out.

His mouth set even more firmly. 'It will be done.'

Laura made her way to the tent set aside for women to powder their noses, and was glad of cold water to bathe her hands. She caught her reflection in the full-sized mirror and did a small twirl. The summer dress fitted her perfectly, even though she'd gained some weight from Mrs Hannacott's fruit crumbles and clotted cream. Like Brendan's, her skin had taken on a glow from the sun, and she saw that her blue eyes sparkled more than they had for a long time.

She skipped out of the ladies' tent straight into the arms of Edward Pascoe. He took hold of her hand.

'Just in time. I've been looking for you. Come on, the music's starting. We can have the first dance together.'

'Yes, but I don't think I can—'

'Now,' he said, tucking her arm into his, and looking at her with mock sternness, 'you gave me your promise. I didn't think you were the sort of woman who went back on her promises.'

'I didn't exactly promise—and certainly not the first dance,' Laura protested, knowing her one concern was how it would look to Brendan. He didn't like Edward, and she didn't want him to think she was betraying him.

'I absolutely insist. It's a polka and I have to dance it with someone light on her feet who'll keep up with me. I will do my duty by the matrons later.'

'And Beatrice too.'

'Ah, the lovely Beatrice. You're not worried about upsetting her? Since when have you two become friends?'

'We're not,' she said shortly, realising he was not going to let her go and short of creating a scene, she could not escape him '. . . But I don't want to make her even more of an . . .'

He laughed. 'Too late for that, I fear,' he said. 'But I'm not promised to her, you know.'

'She's very fond of you, you must know that.'

'She thinks I'm a good catch. But I don't want to talk about other women when I'm dancing with you.'

'I think it's more than that,' Laura told him, but he only shook his head, refusing to be drawn on the subject of Beatrice any further.

He was a good dancer. She was able to relax in his arms and let him steer her round the makeshift floor, while he kept up his teasing flirtatious banter. Beatrice's was not the only unhappy female face she saw following their progress. She glanced at Edward. The knowing look told her that he was enjoying causing a stir. Probably the only reason he'd asked her to dance she thought. Just how far did this man's mischief-making go?

'Colefax is watching us,' he told her. 'Perhaps he's trying to pick up some dancing technique from me.'

Now it was her turn to refuse to be drawn, on the subject of Brendan. She'd avoided looking at him as they moved smoothly round the room. 'You are a good dancer,' she said frankly. 'But then you've had all the advantages of a privileged upbringing.'

He regarded her through narrowed eyes. 'And I think you have too. There's more to you than meets the eye. What secrets are you hiding, Laura? Are you a runaway heiress? And what about Colefax. Just how much do you know about his past?'

The first polka was over, and the band struck up a second. She could not get away from him yet.

'I'm as you see, a secretary earning her living. As for Mr Colefax, he's my employer. I don't need to know about his past.'

'Really? Why don't I believe you? You should ask him about his family.'

'What about your family?' she countered.

What did Edward know of Brendan's secrets? Is that what they quarrelled about? Did Edward have a hold over Brendan? She thought, is he just dancing with me to annoy Brendan?

At last the music stopped and seeing Beatrice heading towards them she made good her escape and made her way to Brendan's side. 'I'm sorry,' she began.

'You couldn't refuse him,' Brendan said quietly. 'And now they're playing a country waltz. Shall we?'

His hand pressing firmly into her back, the other holding her right hand, they moved into the throng. He was not as polished or showy a dancer as Edward, but his lead was strong, and she felt she could relax in his arms too. Was she breaking every convention in the book, dancing with her male employer? She didn't care. For the first time in many years she felt at one with the world and herself.

The evening passed in a blur. Brendan asked several married ladies to dance, whose husbands he knew from Bovey Tracey, and Laura was pleased to be asked by several of the men from Manleigh. She was glad that Edward did not return once Beatrice had captured hold of him. She cast Laura a triumphant glance from her pale green eyes as she sailed by.

In the interval Brendan held out his arm. 'Shall we go outside to cool off?' he suggested.

She put her hand in the crook of his shirt-sleeved arm—it was too hot for the men to keep wearing their jackets—and they strolled outside and away from the entertainment marquee. The air was cool, and filled with moths and flying insects. Above the sky blazed with stars.

'Isn't it beautiful?' she said.

'It is,' he said, turning towards her. His words faltered. Instead he leaned forwards and his lips met hers. She felt his arms go around her, pulling her close. For a moment, she no longer had thoughts or words. There was only the feel of his body against hers, their lips tasting each others' in a lingering kiss. Then Brendan pulled back and she almost shivered, missing his closeness immediately.

'Laura, I'm sorry,' he said, his voice low. 'I should not have overstepped the mark like that. I wish—' he ran his hand through his hair. 'If only . . . there are things, things that I must sort out. I can't make you any promises. You are free. Oh Laura, if only . . .'

They gazed into each other's eyes. Laura's heart ached, but at the same time she felt hope for the first time.

'Come, we'd best go back,' he said, his voice rough. He grasped her hand and they walked quickly back to the marquee.

As they entered the first person they saw was Jed the blacksmith.

'There they are. They're the ones to blame,'

he yelled, his face mottled and red. 'Animals is one thing, now it's innocent old ladies.'

'What are you talking about man?' Brendan demanded.

'Now Jed, she was a very old woman. Perhaps it was her time to pass on,' Farmer Andrew said, laying a hand on Jed's thickly muscled arm. Jed shook him off.

'Gramma Neston had plenty of years in her. You didn't see her, lying on the floor of her cottage.'

All Laura's new-found happiness evaporated. Gramma Neston was dead. Grief gripped her and she was barely aware of the fierce argument that followed, though it stopped short of blows. She allowed herself to be bundled into the cart where she sat waiting with head bowed while Brendan went to find Tom and Mrs Hannacott, both of whom had been absent from the refreshments and dancing. She looked up at the stars, blurred now through tears. What had Gramma said the last time she'd seen her? 'Remember, I'll be watching over you.' It was as if she'd known her time was come, and she'd said goodbye.

CHAPTER EIGHT

Laura found Champion's plod and the creak of the cart soothing as they progressed slowly towards Barton Court Farm. From the front seat she heard the low murmur of conversation between Tom, who was driving, and Brendan. Opposite her in the back, Mrs Hannacott was silent. After she'd contributed the information that she'd been visiting her family, that they'd had words and so she was grateful to be leaving early, she said no more. She didn't ask Laura about her day, and she was glad of that. Abandoned on the floor, beside baskets of goodies bought in such high spirits earlier in the day, lay her 'Best Bonnet'. She felt like stamping on it. Outlined against the stormy sky were Brendan's shoulders, and dark hair. She clenched her hands into fists in her lap to stop herself from reaching out to touch him, the longing to be close to him again was so strong.

Quickly she glanced at Mrs Hannacott. Had she noticed the direction of Laura's gaze? Mrs Hannacott was looking at her, but as her usual expression was one of disgruntled disapproval, it was hard to tell if she'd been able to read Laura's mind or not.

'How did Gramma die?' Laura asked.

'In her own home, just as she'd've wanted.'

'She wasn't ill before? I mean, she didn't suffer . . . I spoke to her only a few days ago. She seemed—' How to explain that she'd seemed resigned, knowing?

Mrs Hannacott shook her head. 'I don't believe she suffered, maid. I expect Gramma knew, anyway. She knew more than just herbs.'

'She had the second sight,' Laura nodded.

'Oh, you've heard about that up in the big city, then.' Mrs Hannacott knew she was from London, but no more than that.

'She didn't have any children.'

'Whatever gave you that idea? She was a widow, and her daughter's married to Andrew. Her knowledge won't be lost.'

'Oh, I thought—she told me she was the last of the Nestons. Of course, her daughter will have Andrew's surname.'

'What in heaven's name—!' Laura heard Brendan exclaim. He stood up in the front. Ahead, there was a glow in the night sky.

'I think that's fire!' he said. 'Quick Tom, we'll run ahead. Laura, take the reins.'

In a matter of moments he and Tom were running up the rise and disappearing over the top. Laura scrambled over the backboard and took up the reins and urged Champion into a faster walk. Behind her she was sure she heard Mrs Hannacott say, 'I knew it, I knew it.' But was her tone regretful or triumphant?

The flames had taken quite a hold on the laboratory. Laura saw billowing smoke carrying sparks up into the air, and above the roaring of the fire she could hear delicate glass flasks and tubes exploding inside.

'Laura, Mrs Hannacott, you'll have to help us,' Brendan called. 'Tom's pumping the water, make a chain to pass the buckets to and fro, we must try and put it out.'

'Place is tinder dry,' Mrs Hannacott muttered as they passed full and empty buckets to each other as fast as they could. Mrs Hannacott took from Tom, and Laura passed her full buckets to Brendan who threw them on the fire. 'And the Lord knows what he's got in there. All them chemicals. Whole place will explode.'

If you don't be quiet, I'll explode, Laura thought, trying to ignore her. Were they winning? At least it seemed that her office was unaffected. The fire seemed to be concentrated at the far end of the lab.

'I'm going to try and break in,' Brendan shouted to her. 'If I can clear stuff to the far end—if I can find the chemical I want I may be able to dowse the flames. Throw the last bucket over me!'

Laura did as he said, drenching him head to foot with water. His dark hair was plastered to his head, his shirt clung to his chest. He held a strip of sacking over his face then ran at the lab door, drop kicking it open with one blow of his foot.

'Be careful,' Laura called as he disappeared inside. Should she have tried to stop him? Would he be safe? Her heart was in her mouth as the three redoubled their efforts, coughing and with eyes streaming. After a few minutes, which seemed to Laura the longest she'd ever known, he reappeared in the doorway streaked with soot and smoke. Behind him the fire was already calmer, the flames dying down.

Laura couldn't stop herself giving a half sob and tears welled up in her eyes. He was safe! Arms and legs trembling with effort now the worst seemed to be over, she continued to pass buckets until Brendan said, 'I think we can rest for a bit. Tom, you and I need to shovel some earth on to the flames, can you get a barrowload from the vegetable patch?'

Tom gave a nod in reply and trotted away around the side of the farmhouse.

'Good thing whoever set the fire didn't know what they were doing,' Brendan said. 'Come and look.'

They followed him over the yard to the far end of the laboratory, the opposite end to her office. Laura could feel heat radiating from the stone walls, and coughed as acrid smoke caught at her throat. Against the outside wall Brendan showed them the remains of a bonfire. 'Must've set the fire here.'

'If they'd broken in they could've done much more damage,' Laura said.

'Too frightened more like,' Mrs Hannacott said. 'Probably thinking about all the sickness and chemicals they're afraid you got in there.'

'There's no "sickness" in there, as you put it Mrs Hannacott, as you very well know, ' Brendan sighed.

'I knows that but they don't, do 'em?' she retorted. 'If you don't need me, I'll go and put the kettle on, make some tea.'

'I didn't mean to upset her,' Brendan said as they watched her stomp across the yard followed by Tom, who'd set the barrow of earth down by the laboratory door.

'It must've been Jed who did this—only he was with us, at the Fair. He must've sent someone else. Oh Brendan, I'm so sorry. All your work.' She gestured helplessly.

'Don't be. The important part—your office—is safe. All the notes and results are in there. The material for the papers I intend to write—all safe.' He sounded almost cheerful

'Does that mean your experiments are over?'

'The current set, yes.'

'You didn't tell me.' She was surprised at how hurt she felt and sounded.

He took her by the shoulders. 'Look at me Laura.' She met his gaze, trying not to feel distracted by the touch of his fingers. 'There is a reason for not telling you everything. Will you trust me a little longer on that? Though, heaven knows, I could understand why you—' Abruptly he let her go and turned to survey the wreckage. 'It can all be rebuilt, brought into use again. If I can persuade the bank manager to give me a loan. Do you want to come and check the office?'

They checked that the papers were safe, and that there was no further danger of sparks setting them alight. She stepped outside while Brendan locked the office door. Something—a movement—caught the corner of her eye. She strained her eyes, looking into the trees and bushes beyond the farmyard. Yes, there—wasn't that the girl she'd seen the night of her arrival? Pale face, long chemise-like gown.

'Brendan,' she called urgently. 'Look—look, it's her. The lost child.'

He arrived beside her. 'I'm sorry, I don't see anything,' he said. Laura blinked. Neither could she, now. 'Perhaps she's a Romany child, living in the woods—wanted to see what the fire was all about,' he added kindly.

I can't blame him for not believing me, Laura thought. It's only me that ever sees her. And if Gramma Neston hadn't known what I was talking about, I would just believe I was seeing ghosts.

*   *   *

'. . . I'm so sorry that I have been neglectful of you. And there are things that I should have told you, but I kept putting it off, waiting for the right moment. It hardly seems any time since you were a young girl—how the years have flown. I admire your resourcefulness and I am glad that the tuition I have provided for you, the example I have set, have helped you in these difficult times. I am making arrangements right now to come to you—I hope it will be only a couple of weeks before we see each other again. Your loving Aunt,

Rose. PS below are some of my latest adventures, in case you can bear to read them.'

There followed some delightful pen and ink drawings of scenes, some with people, some of plants and animals, each annotated. Laura smiled fondly. This was one of the reasons she'd kept all her aunt's letters over the years, rereading them until she felt she'd actually been to these places too. She'd had to leave them behind, in the tin trunk in her old bedroom. They've probably thrown it out, she thought sadly. Or forced the trunk open and burned the contents.

She folded the letter and put it to one side on her desk, then turned to the typewriter once more. Beside her were some particularly complex notes—Brendan must've written them up late at night, as his handwriting was especially squiggly. She brushed her fingertips over the lines he'd written, feeling pleasure at even this second-hand connection with him. But she was more expert at deciphering his notes now, and was also beginning to form a picture about the direction of his research. If he was successful, then he would help in alleviating an illness that was a scourge of so many, and which she'd seen first-hand for herself in the drawing-rooms, as well as in the poorer streets, of London.

She heard a thump and a crack from next door followed by a muffled angry response from Brendan. She smiled. He was refitting the laboratory—or as much as he needed at this tail end of his work. It was not proving straightforward. The smell of burnt wood and scorched materials still lingered in the air.

She began to type. Tail end of his work. She refused to think about that, or what might lie beyond. She would take each day as it came and enjoy the time she had with him as much as she could. He'd asked her to trust him, and she would, whatever the outcome. She almost—but not quite—wished he hadn't pulled her into his arms and kissed her because now she was certain how she felt about him. But she had the imminent arrival of her Aunt to look forward to and to distract her.

Tom had brought the letter from Manleigh Post Office. In the weeks since the fire, Laura had decided not to go to the village. She feared she might speak out too angrily against those she was sure had set the fire. Jed's may not have been the hand that lit the fire, but whoever had done it, had done it at his bidding. She was sure of that.

She also hadn't wanted to leave Brendan and Mrs Hannacott on their own. Though what protection I would be, I don't know, she thought. I suppose I could always get on my bike and pedal to Hamholt where the nearest Police Station was. A constable had come to Barton Court after the fire and taken notes, but she doubted he would be doing anything

99

about it. For all they knew, he could be related to the Manleigh villagers.

Tom had brought other news too. Today was Gramma Newton's funeral. It had taken place that morning.

'Do you want to go?' Brendan had asked, as they sat around the kitchen table. Laura shook her head.

'I don't think it would be wise,' she said.

'Red rag to a bull,' Mrs Hannacott agreed, 'Best let things simmer down. My sister'll be going, so that'll do for me.'

'Thank you,' Brendan said quietly. He looked exhausted, dark shadows under his eyes, his hands pink and peeling from superficial burns. Every morning and evening he allowed her to gently rub salve into them, and she enjoyed being able to do something for him. If only Gramma was still with them, she would have had remedies to give him too.

After breakfast Laura had walked down to the stream where she'd spent such a carefree afternoon with Brendan, picking wildflowers as she went. Casting them into the water, she made her own personal farewell to Gramma, and thought she could hear the old woman's chuckle of approval. And with that came an understanding. The ghostly young girl—that had been a message for Gramma that her time was near. Only being nearly blind she wouldn't have seen her. It had been Laura's duty to pass on the message . . .

She'd shaken herself. Where had that fanciful idea come from? But as she had walked through the woods back to the farm, she had felt a strong sense of peace.

What was that? The sound of chanting? And heavy boots? Shocked, she jumped up and looked out of her window. What she saw made her heart thump with fear. A group of maybe ten or fifteen people were coming through the gateway into the old farmyard. Their expressions were wild and fierce. They were shouting loudly, and they carried pots and pans and short sticks. Among the men were several women, looking as tough as their menfolk. And at their head marched Jed Parr the Blacksmith.

Quickly she ran into the laboratory, to find Brendan already moving to the door.

'Stay in your office, Laura. Lock the door,' he ordered.

'I will not. I'm with you,' she declared.

His face softened and he held out his hand as if to take hers, then pulled it back. 'Please Laura, I couldn't bear it if any harm came to you.'

'Nor I you.' Their eyes met. He gave a small nod.

'Very well, shall we greet our visitors—together?'

Brendan stepped out in to the yard, Laura close behind him. The group from the village came to a ragged standstill, and fell quiet.

Then Jed took one pace forwards.

'Today,' he intoned loudly, 'We buried one of our own. An innocent old woman who should not have died. Who will be next? Will it be a mother, a brother, a sister? Or one of our children?'

There were some murmurs of encouragement from his 'gang'.

'How many animals have caught the mysterious sickness and died now? Every death taking food from our mouths.' The murmurs became louder.

'We know whose fault that is, don't we?' The murmurs died down again and the villagers shuffled their feet.

'Don't we!' he roared, forcing agreement from his followers. 'We've given enough messages—we want you gone, Colefax, before you bring any more trouble on the village. Give it to them!'

At this he started to bang the big pot he carried with a stick and the others followed suit, making a terrible racket. Laura saw Mrs Hannacott come out onto the kitchen doorstep.

Brendan held up his hand and the noise stopped, Jed giving his pot one final thwack. 'I can promise you that I have not caused the deaths of any of your animals, nor the death of Gramma Newton. I have sent away some samples to the top scientists at Cambridge, and I expect the results any day now. Then, and only then, will we know what—or who—is causing your animals to die.'

'Rubbish,' Jed yelled, moving forward another pace. 'All lies. We won't believe anything you've made up with your friends in Cambridge. Do anything you ask if pay 'em enough, am I right?'

A chorus of yeses was accompanied by clangs and shouted agreement.

'How can you say that?' Laura declared hotly. 'Mr Colefax is honest—he wouldn't lie to you. He's trying to help, can't you see?'

Farmer Andrew spoke up. 'We don't hold anything against you Miss, even your bike riding. You're a brave maid. But this is just between us and Colefax.'

'I'm sorry Miss Laura,' his wife chimed in. Gramma Neston's daughter, Laura thought. Surely she could be made to see reason? 'It do look as if Colefax brought this trouble. It only started when he arrived.'

'And now he's got to go!'

The crowd advanced another step, renewing their clanging and battering.

'Enough!' Mrs Hannacott's voice could barely be heard, and she clapped her hands to get attention. 'You lot, you should be ashamed of yourselves. I watched while Mr Colefax took his samples—not a pretty sight neither—and made sure 'em was packed and sealed and sent off to that there Cambridge myself. You'll take my word for it when the results come they'll be true.'

The banging stopped and everyone looked at Jed, who seemed to swell up with annoyance.

'We know Amy, she wouldn't lie to us,' one man said, and the others joined him.

'Amy would speak true,' Gramma Neston's daughter agreed.

'What Mrs Hannacott says is the truth,' Brendan told them. 'All I'm asking is for a few days, until we get the results. Then we'll have a meeting. I have my suspicions, but if I'm wrong then I'm willing to listen to you. All right?' he said, deliberately holding out his hand to Jed.

'Go on,' Farmer Andrew said, shoving Jed forward. Reluctantly, the blacksmith took Brendan's hand for a moment, then dropped it like a hot cake. Slowly the group turned around and began walking along the path back to the village, debating fiercely among themselves.

Laura let out a shaky breath. What would have happened if Mrs Hannacott hadn't spoken up?

'Thank you Laura, Mrs Hannacott,' Brendan said. 'I think we need a cup of tea— or even a glass of medicinal brandy.' He turned to Laura. 'I had to keep it secret—I knew the villagers would only take Mrs Hannacott's word. I didn't want you to be put in a compromising position if they tried to get information out of you, or try to threaten you.'

She nodded, 'I think I understand. Now we have to wait for the results. What do you think they will say?'

He shook his head. 'Again, I think you'll be safer if you don't know. That must have been obvious to anyone watching you this afternoon. Come on, let's lock up and go on in. I don't know about you but all that shouting has put me off work for now.'

As she covered her typewriter and picked up her Aunt's letter, she wondered where Tom had been. He'd been conspicuous by his absence, just when they needed him. And if push had come to shove, whose side would he be on anyway?

CHAPTER NINE

Laura lifted her feet from the pedals and let her bicycle freewheel down the dip, allowing the momentum to carry her up the next hill, until she had to begin pedalling furiously to get to the very top, where she knew the land at last levelled off. Would the package that she and Brendan so eagerly awaited be at the station today, she wondered? The results from the scientists in Cambridge which Jed seemed so intent on denying.

Brendan had announced at breakfast that he was going to Hamholt Station himself.

Immediately Laura had said, 'Please let me go. I've not been anywhere for several weeks. I really want to get out on my bike again.'

'I don't know,' Brendan said, frowning. 'It's a long way—'

'I've cycled that distance before.'

'I know, but it's a long way to go by yourself, especially as all of Manleigh must be aware the results are coming any day soon. I wouldn't put it past one of them trying to get hold of them. We know from Tom what Jed's been up to.'

'Telling everyone that the results can't be trusted, I know. But I won't be going anywhere near the village and if I see anyone from Manleigh I'll hide behind a bush.'

Brendan smiled but still looked doubtful. 'We could go together, if one of us didn't need to be here to look after the place.'

'Besides, I want to tell the stationmaster that my Aunt Rose will be arriving any day now,' Laura added her most persuasive argument.

'Very well,' he'd conceded. 'But don't take any risks. I don't want anything to happen to you.' Then, to make light of his remark, he said, 'You're far too valuable a typist for that.'

She smiled, remembering the shared joke as she crested the rise, reliving the look in his eyes, the curve of his mouth—

Something slammed into the side of her. With a cry she crashed to the ground, her legs tangled up in her machine. For a moment, she couldn't breathe as all the air had been knocked from her lungs. As she thrashed with her legs something was thrown over her head, suffocating her. In the blackness she struggled even harder, lashing out with hands and feet, trying to scream as loudly as she could, then choking on the musty dust from whatever had enveloped her. An old sack?

Strong hands grabbed hers and forced them to her sides, and she felt a rope being passed around her body, then being pulled tight. She had no chance of escaping as the rope was twisted once round her ankles, though she did manage to land a kick from her booted foot, judging from the exclamation she heard. Then, trussed like a chicken, she was picked up and slung unceremoniously over her captor's shoulder. He began to walk, ignoring her struggles and muffled cries. She guessed he was moving into the woods, as she heard twigs cracking and felt the brush of branches.

'Jed,' she tried to say—because it had to be Jed. 'Stop this. Let me go . . .' But even to her own ears all that came out was muffled nonsense. She let herself go limp and as heavy as she could. She would save all her strength to fight back when they arrived at whatever was her destination. The man who'd kidnapped her took no notice of her anyway. He continued to stride forward as if she was nothing more than a sack of potatoes.

She tried to listen out for sounds that might give her a clue about which way they were going but could make nothing out but the swish of leaves and the singing of birds. Instead, she began to feel very uncomfortable and dizzy, bumping along upside-down. The dust in the sacking tickled her nose and she sneezed and then coughed again. The man who was carrying her ignored her.

After what seemed about twenty minutes but could have been shorter—or longer—he stopped and she heard a rattle. She guessed it was the sound of a bolt or a latch. She prepared herself to launch an attack on him as soon as she was freed. But he levered her from his shoulder and dropped her on the ground. She felt a tug on the rope and as it fell away she tried to struggle up but the sacking got in her way. As she pulled it from her head with one hand, lashing out with the other, she heard the rattle again.

She looked around. She was alone in some sort of small hut or shed. The floor was beaten earth and above her were rafters and tiles, all festooned with cobwebs. In front of her were a door and a small very grimy window. She clambered to her feet and ran to the door but as she had already guessed, it was firmly locked.

She peered through the window. 'Jed,' she shouted. 'Don't leave me here. This won't do any good. Jed!'

The window was so filthy she could barely make out anything through it. She spat on her handkerchief and rubbed at the glass. Outside she could see nothing but grass, trees and bushes. This shed had perhaps been built for woodcutters or charcoal burners, she thought. Only a local person would know it existed and it seemed to be miles from any habitation.

She tried calling and shouting again for a while, but the only result was a sore throat. 'Think,' she said to herself. 'Is there anything I can use to break the window? What do I have on me?'

But apart from her handkerchief she had nothing. She didn't even have a key to the farm. Someone was always there to let her in. The few pennies she carried had fallen out when she was seized. 'Not even a hatpin to pick the lock,' she sighed.

Carefully she searched the small hut. In one corner were some pieces of wood which were so dry they crumbled when she picked them up. She felt the walls. Not even a stone loose.

What about her shoes? She unlaced one and tried hammering at the window but the leather was too soft to make an impact. Anyway, the panes were so small she wouldn't be able to escape that way.

She spread the sacking on the floor, sat down and put her shoes back on. At least it wasn't cold and there didn't appear to be any rats or mice—yet. She clasped her arms over her knees. When would Brendan discover that she was missing and come to look for her? Would he be the first to find her bicycle in the road, or had Jed gone to hide it?

She bowed her head and closed her eyes. If only she hadn't insisted on riding to Hamholt. Brendan had tried to persuade her not to. He was right and she was wrong. Now she'd simply caused him more trouble when he least needed it.

But why had Jed kidnapped her? Did he want her out of the way so that he could attack the farm again? Or was he going to use her to blackmail Brendan in some way. And how had he known she was setting off for the station alone? It could only be one man who'd told him—Tom. Always lurking about in the bushes. She was sure now that he was Jed's informant and Brendan was entirely wrong to trust him.

She sighed. Nothing for it but to wait till someone came. She began to feel the aches and pains of cuts and bruises. Don't be too long, Brendan, she thought.

She must have dozed for a while. She came to thinking she could hear voices. She strained her ears. Yes! A man's voice—and then another.

Stiffly she clambered to her feet and went to the window and squinted out. A man was standing at the edge of the clearing with his back to her. He was of slight build and wore a black coat with a hat covering his hair. There was something familiar about the set of his shoulders. Edward Pascoe? No, he was taller. All the same . . . In front of him stood a much bigger and more thickset man. He was bareheaded, his hair close-cropped and he wore a working man's clothes. He had to be the one who'd snatched her from her bicycle.

The man in the coat appeared to be angry with him by the way he gesticulated. But the other merely shrugged and stuck out his hand. He would not give ground and eventually the man in the coat put his hand in his pocket and handed something over. Money, Laura calculated. The big man thrust the money in his pocket and turned and left without another word.

Laura found she was holding her breath. She'd never seen the big man before, and the man in the black coat was not Jed. So who had orchestrated her kidnap? He turned, and it was the last person she expected to see.

'Cousin Horace! What on earth are you doing?' Suddenly furious she banged on the window pane. 'Let me out of here this instant. How dare you take me prisoner?'

He walked toward the hut but halted a few paces away as if keeping himself out of her range, despite the fact that she was caged up.

'Laura,' he said then stopped.

'Does Cousin Venetia know where you are and what you've done?' she demanded.

'I—' he began, then stopped again.

'And who was that man? Did you tell him to knock me off my bike? I hope it isn't damaged,' she heard herself say.

'Now look here Laura, be quiet,' he said, regaining some of his usual command under her onslaught. 'Listen to me. I must admit I did not know his methods were going to be so, er, extreme. I'm sorry for that. But desperate times demand desperate measures.'

She recalled that he had been remonstrating with the man. 'What desperate time?' she asked. 'I'm the one in a desperate position.'

He stepped forward and adopted the stern, lecturing tone she remembered from her younger years. 'You've done a very wicked thing, Laura, running away—absconding—from a loving home. Venetia was very upset. Many's the night she's cried herself to sleep.'

Not sure whether to believe him that Venetia had shed actual tears, nonetheless she felt a worm of guilt. 'I'm sorry for that but you left me no choice. I knew what you were planning for my future and that you would leave me no way out.'

Now he was closer she could see there were new lines on his face and a haunted look in his eyes she'd not seen before. But he wasn't backing down.

'Ungrateful girl. We took you in and looked after you, fed you and clothed you, gave you a good education, for all those years—'

112

'I think Aunt Rose made sure you had money enough for that,' she said drily.

'Your sainted Aunt Rose was only too happy to pass responsibility for you to us. You wanted for nothing and your cousins once removed were like brothers and sisters to you.'

'It's true I wanted for nothing, and it's not your or Cousin Venetia's fault that I—I didn't quite fit in. But that's in the past—it's the plot you were hatching about my future that I—'

'We were thinking of you.' Horace raised his voice and took another step forward. She could see now how worn the collar of his coat was, and that his shirt was not its usual starched perfection. Even his shoes were rubbed and old. What had been going on since she left? 'A safe and comfortable future. Being married to Stillington meant you'd have wanted for nothing.'

'And from what I overheard, neither would you. You were selling me—he was going to pay you handsomely for me. Ugh,' she shuddered, and for the first time betrayed her hurt, 'Was he the highest bidder? Is that why you took me in? All those years you were just—just fattening me up for the market!'

'No!' His voice was turning shrill. 'Never. It was he who came to us. He saw you at a Ball. And it was the answer to our prayers. Now Laura, listen to me, we are your guardians. We stand in loco parentis and we insist that you marry him.'

'I will not,' she said firmly. 'He's forty years older than me, I don't love him and—even beyond those things, it's the principle. I won't be sold, like your stocks and shares.'

'Principles be hanged. There's more at stake here,' his voice was still shrill. 'I have the key to your prison.' He held it up to show her. 'And you'll stay in there till you submit and sign this paper to prove it.' He pulled a piece of paper from his pocket with his other hand and waved it at her.

'What happens if I refuse?' she said, becoming aware that someone was approaching through the trees. Not the big man, back for more money?

'Then—then—I'll fetch a judge,' Horace said. 'It's your legal duty to—to—'

Tom stepped out of the trees. Laura's heart skipped a beat. Was he alone? Whose side was he on? Horace saw her eyes widen and turned round.

'Be off fellow,' he ordered. 'This is none of your business.'

'She's here Master Colefax,' Tom called, breaking into a brief smile.

'Go away,' Horace shouted. 'This is my ward, my cousin-in-law and I have every right to chastise her.'

Brendan appeared behind Tom. Laura's heart quickened its beat and she heard herself cry out in delight. He strode over to Horace and held out his hand. 'Brendan Colefax,' he said easily. 'Miss Crestwood is in my employ and in my care now. Who are you?' He was a good head taller than Horace, who seemed to shrink down into his clothes like a tortoise into its shell. Tom waited a few paces behind Brendan.

'Horace Middleship.' Gingerly he took Brendan's hand and shook it. 'Laura is my ward but she refuses to obey us. It's her bounden duty to obey me and marry as I direct her.'

Brendan looked over at her. 'Laura, why are you hiding in that shed? Are you frightened of Mr Middleship?'

'Not at all,' she said indignantly. 'He's locked me in.'

'The key please.' Brendan held out his hand again.

'No, you can't have it.' Horace closed his hand into a fist on the key and thrust it into his pocket. 'You don't understand. Laura has to do what we want. It's the only way—we can't survive—we'll be ruined—our name in the mud . . .' he was babbling in desperation, hardly making any sense. Brendan patted him on the shoulder then turned to Tom.

'Can you break the door down?'

' 'Course. We keeps an axe round the back.'

Two minutes later a couple of blows from Tom's axe splintered the door enough to allow Laura to climb through and she was free. Horace was now weeping, his head in his

115

hands, a broken man.

Brendan strode forward and pulled Laura into a tight embrace. 'Thank God,' he whispered into her hair. 'Are you hurt?' He pulled away and looked at her. 'What happened? Your bike was found by Farmer Andrew who was moving his cows to another field. He came and told us right away. Tom here followed tracks that led through the woods, we hoped they might be yours.'

Still in his arms she gazed up, drinking in his face. 'Someone grabbed me from my bike. At first I thought it must be Jed. He put a sack over my head and tied my arms down. He carried me over his shoulder.' She found she was trembling. 'Later I saw this big man talking to Horace, it wasn't anyone I recognised. I saw Horace give him money.' She glanced over at Horace who stood quietly now, looking completely dejected.

'I'll tell you everything,' she said. 'No more secrets. This really is my distant cousin and when I was orphaned I did live in his house. He's a banker but,' she bit her lip, 'I think he has been hiding much from me and he has plenty to reveal.'

Brendan pulled her close again in reassurance. 'Whatever his plans, you're safe now. You have friends in your corner.'

'And Aunt Rose is coming soon—oh, we haven't collected your results from the station!'

'Time enough to talk about that. Let's get you home and see to any cuts and bruises.' He wasn't letting her go. 'Can you walk through the woods back to the road?' She nodded. 'Good. Tom, bring Mr Middleship will you?' Holding her hand tightly he ushered her away from the woodcutter's hut. The feel of his hand on hers miraculously banished all her aches and pains from her mind.

CHAPTER TEN

'Look,' Laura said as they turned into the familiar driveway to Barton Court Farm. 'Is that clouds? Does that mean we're going to get rain at last and an end to this heat?'

Brendan grinned. 'Contrary to popular belief I don't understand the weather or what drives it. But those clouds do look promising. It's a long time since we've seen any—that was the night you arrived, the night of the big storm.'

They were sitting side by side in the back of Farmer Andrew's trap. Laura had been very relieved to find him waiting for them in the lane when they emerged from the woods. Her legs had started to feel very wobbly from delayed shock. Horace sat silently in the front between Tom and Andrew, head bowed. Was he truly sorry or would he start ordering her about again once they arrived?

They swung into the yard and immediately the back door opened and in the next moment she was jumping down and running into the arms of Aunt Rose. They hugged for a long time, and then Aunt Rose stepped back. 'Let me look at your properly. My but you're bonny and all grown up—good heavens, is that Horace? What's he doing here? And what happened? I surmised you must have fallen off your bike and wandered off in a daze. I've been telling myself off roundly for ensuring you learned to ride the dratted things. Meanwhile, Mrs Hannacott has been filling me in on what's been happening here.'

As Horace walked past them without a word, Tom holding his arm, Aunt Rose drew Laura to her. 'We can speak later. Come on, Mrs Hannacott has got the kettle on. You need a wash and a cup of tea. I always feel better when we've set up camp somewhere in the wilderness and have got a fire going.' Laura allowed her aunt to take charge of her, chattering as she did so. Her skin was freckled by hot suns, the hair that escaped her bonnet was sunbleached, and she was beginning to look her age, but her eyes were as bright and lively as ever.

At last Laura was able to sit at the big farmhouse table with Brendan, Aunt Rose and Horace. Farmer Andrew and Tom sat on a wooden settle by the range while Mrs

Hannacott was busy cutting more fruitcake which Aunt Rose was eating with great relish. 'There are just a few things I really miss about England, and good home-made fruitcake is one of them. Now Laura, if you can, tell me everything. It seems Horace has been struck dumb at the moment.'

As Laura recounted her tale she found she was making light of it. Something in Horace's demeanour was making her feel sorry for him. When she finished, they all stared at him.

'Horace!' Aunt Rose said loudly, slapping her hand on the table and making them all jump. 'Pull yourself together, man, and speak!'

'Ruined,' he said faintly. 'We're ruined. The bank . . . no more money.' He closed his eyes in shame.

'How on earth have you managed to run the bank into the ground?' Aunt Rose asked.

He shook his head. 'Speculation. It all sounded so plausible. An expedition to Alaska, millions to be made in minerals and gold. I put everything in it, and when the reports started coming back about rich finds I put the customers' deposits in too. I thought we'd all be very rich. But it was all a con, a fraud. No mines, no minerals, no gold.'

'But if they kept drilling, surely something would've been found. I've heard Alaska is a rich source for mining,' Brendan said.

'There wasn't even an expedition,' Horace said faintly, shaking his head. 'I began borrowing to cover up and keep paying the shareholders, anything to avoid the horror of collapse. Then Stillington came to me. Somehow he'd got wind of the fraud. He said he could put enough money in to keep the bank afloat till I—till we were viable again.'

'And in return he wanted to marry me?'

'As I told you, he'd've provided for you very well, Laura. At the time it seemed the perfect solution. Only—'

'Only I found out and vanished. He must still want to marry me, I suppose, or you wouldn't've come to find me. Am I that big a prize? A man like him could have any young woman he wanted, and some might have jumped at the chance. So why me?' She frowned. 'I only met him a couple of times. Why was he so taken with me?'

Aunt Rose sighed. 'I know why. In a year's time you come into your inheritance.'

'But that's only a few hundred pounds. It's nothing to a man like him.'

'There are a few share certificates your father picked up when he was working in South Africa. Funnily enough, they are mining shares. Virtually worthless until two years ago, when they struck the most incredible seam of diamonds. They could be worth a great deal now. Hmm,' she looked thoughtfully at Horace. 'Stillington must have heard about those shares. Horace, you didn't happen to tell him did you?'

120

Horace coloured. 'I might have let something slip.'

Aunt Rose made a sound of exasperation. 'You hooked him Horace. You baited the hook and reeled him in with the promise of yet more money.'

'But I would have made sure he didn't neglect Laura. Don't you see? He had to leave all his money in my bank. Venetia and I would have had a say,' he pleaded.

Rose ignored him. 'Laura, this is all my fault. I should've told you about those shares gaining value. But it was all so recent and they might have fallen again. I decided to wait and hope it would be a wonderful surprise on your twenty-first birthday. I didn't want to raise, then dash, your hopes. Now we have to decide what to do.'

'What to do?' Horace echoed her, sounding alarmed.

'I'll go back to London with you to look over Laura's affairs and make sure everything is in order. And maybe I can pull in a favour or two, see if we can find a legitimate purchaser for the bank. You will have to either retire, Horace, or learn to dance to someone else's tune.'

'One thing,' Laura said, finally locating the question that had been nagging at her. 'How did you find out where I was, Horace?'

'I had a letter from a friend of yours, Beatrice Huntingdon. She said she was worried about you and felt we should come and find you. She gave us your address. I made enquiries, and that's when we decided we had to do this. Desperate measures I said Laura—in two days' time we have a shareholder's meeting and then everything will come out.'

Laura was no longer listening. Beatrice! She remembered her looking over her shoulder at the address on the envelope when she was posting her letter to Aunt Rose in the post office in Manleigh. She would have asked around and it would be easy to follow the trail back to London and the Middleships. Trust her to stir up trouble in order to keep rivals away from Edward Pascoe.

'Will you come with us, Laura?' Aunt Rose asked.

Laura didn't need to pause to think. 'No thanks—at least, not yet.' Her eyes sought Brendan's. He'd been sitting quietly, listening to everything that was said. 'My work here isn't finished yet.'

'You can leave if you want to Laura. If you want to go with your Aunt,' he said.

'I can't possibly go before finding out the results of all your work,' she told him.

'Amy—Mrs Hannacott—has been trying to explain to me what exactly you are working on, Mr Colefax, but I still don't seem to understand,' Aunt Rose said.

'The main thrust of my research and explorations I have been keeping secret. Partly to protect everyone—the less they know, the less problems they might encounter. And also so that when I publish my findings, perhaps even give an account of them at the Royal Society, it will be fresh news and no one will have a chance to sabotage my work. Of course, here in Manleigh, we have encountered problems.'

Mrs Hannacott and Tom started speaking then at the same time as Brendan, each wanting to give their account of the fire, and the other encounters they'd suffered. Then Brendan held up his hand. 'I can now reveal what's caused the death of some of the animals in the village.' He took a folded letter from his waistcoat pocket. 'The results from Cambridge did arrive today. In fact the stationmaster gave my letter to his trusted deputy, who then encountered Tom on the road and—'

'Never mind how it got here,' Laura exclaimed. 'What does it say?'

'As I have suspected for some time now. The poor animals have been poisoned. With Tom's help I had been able to pinpoint which animals drank at which water troughs, and take samples of the water. The analysis of the water, along with the blood from your pig, Andrew, shows a nasty poison. Someone in the village has been poisoning animals and trying to blacken my name.'

Farmer Andrew jumped to his feet, his face red with anger. 'I'll get 'em for this—'

' 'Twas Jed,' Tom spoke up. 'I saw him with my own eyes and I told Mr Colefax, but he had to have his proof. And we know why don't we?'

Andrew subsided onto the settle again. 'Jed—of course. No wonder he was always going on about Mr Colefax. So it must be here that he—only I wasn't sure if it was just rumours.'

'Aye,' said Tom. 'He wanted Mr Colefax gone so that he could have use of the deserted farm again, well away from prying eyes.'

'What for?' Laura asked.

'Jed trades in racehorses, ones that aren't his, if you take my meaning. Had to hide them away somewhere. We thought it was just a bit of fun, cocking a snook at the police, but now it's gone too far,' Andrew said. He stood up again. 'I'll deal with this. Coming Tom? We need to pay Mr Pascoe Senior a visit. He's Justice of the Peace around here.'

'I knew it,' Mrs Hannacott said. 'My sister wouldn't believe me but I told her Mr Colefax was a good man. We had a terrible row day of the Fair. She'll have to ask my pardon now. I shall be waiting for it,' she said with a sniff.

Once Tom and Andrew had left, and Horace had been allowed to go into another room to lie down as he said his head was aching, Aunt Rose turned to Brendan and asked, 'What has been so important to you that you've risked everything for it, young

124

man.'

He took a deep breath. 'Tuberculosis is the greatest cause of illness and death that we have in this country,' he told them. 'All sorts of cures have been tried, but it's proved intractable. We've conquered smallpox, curbed typhoid, but not TB. A few years ago a Dr Trudeau devised a regime of fresh air, healthy diet, and rest. No one believed in his methods, which were based on earlier work by a Dr Boddington—except me. I've been testing various chemicals and cures to finally eliminate them, proving a negative, if you like, and drawing all the evidence together. And I also want to open a sanatorium near Bovey Tracey and try out my theories. The air is very pure here, coming down from the Moors.

'So to answer your question yes, I hope Laura can stay a few more days, then my work will be finished.'

*　　　*　　　*

Laura lay in bed and listened to the rain thundering on the roof and gurgling in the gutters. She snuggled down under her feather eiderdown. Just a few minutes more, she thought. Then I'll get up and face the world.

It seemed strange not to have a reason to get up, and not to have a time to start work. Three days ago she'd finished typing up the last of Brendan's work. He had asked her to read through and correct by hand. Then he'd disappeared across the yard into the farmhouse. When Laura finished and went indoors Mrs Hannacott told her it would be just the two of them for supper.

'Mr Colefax said he was going up country,' she said. 'He didn't tell me any more nor that.'

'Oh,' Laura said. They looked at one another. Mrs Hannacott gave an unexpected nod of sympathy.

'There there. That's men for you.'

'He didn't say anything about when he'd be back?'

'No, I'm sorry my dear, I don't know any more than you do.'

At first Laura assumed he was making arrangements to open the sanitorium, perhaps in Exeter. But gossip filtered back that he'd gone further away.

Heavy-hearted, Laura forced herself to get out of bed. As always, she went to the window and looked out. A shroud of cloud and mist hung over the hills and the sky was a sheet of grey cloud. Deep puddles stood in the farmyard and there was a flush of new grass and leaves on the trees. She sighed. The rain was good for the land and would wash away the last of the poison Jed had laid. And it was easier to sleep in the cool nights. She sighed again.

She couldn't delay any longer. Since Brendan left she'd eked out her last work of revising and checking, but she couldn't pretend any more. Her work here was done. There was no longer any reason for her to stay. She turned and looked at her few possessions. It wouldn't take long to pack them. But first she'd dress and go down to have one last breakfast. She'd already arranged for Tom to come and take her to the station this morning.

Sighing she washed and dressed. If only Brendan had said something before he left. Given her even the smallest hint that he wanted her to stay until he returned. But he'd ridden away without a word. She paused for a moment to look at her reflection one last time in the fragment of fly-spotted mirror, reliving the moment as she had done many times already, when he'd held her close after releasing her from the hut.

She'd been sure then that he felt the same for her as she did for him. She couldn't deny it any more. She'd fallen in love with him. He'd shown such tenderness and care for her and she'd thought they'd shared an understanding. Well, she wasn't the first woman to make that mistake.

She'd waited for him to say something, make a declaration, through the next day, and then the one after, but he returned to his friendly distance.

She reached the conclusion that she'd been wrong and that he had no long term intentions towards her. He might be . . . fond of her, but his ambitions lay elsewhere. It was best that she move on rather than prolong the agony of hope and her heart broke even more. Now she squared her shoulders. Time to face the world.

After that everything seemed to happen very fast. Mrs Hannacott gave her a hug and a basket of goodies for the train, including some of her fruitcake and her sister's famed rhubarb jam. 'Your Aunt said they was the best she'd ever tasted, even though she's travelled the world and all.' The two women had got along famously, Laura knew. 'Now, look after yourself.' She waved as Tom urged Champion out of the yard and on the way to Hamholt Station. The last thing Laura saw was her bicycle leaning against the wall. Laura swallowed the lump in her throat.

As they passed the spot where Laura had seen the girl in white she thought back to a conversation she'd had with Gramma Neston's daughter Mary, Farmer Andrew's wife. Laura had visited her yesterday with some gifts from Mrs Hannacott, and had asked her about the strange girl. 'Gramma seemed to know who she was,' she said.

Mary nodded. 'There is an old legend about a changeling child that appears when something's going to happen, but I heard there was a Romany encampment not far away. More like one of their children.'

Laura had opened her mouth to share with

128

Mary the notion that had come to her at the riverbank when she'd made her own private farewell to Gramma, but something in Mary's expression had made her close it again. If that was the truth, it was something that should not be talked about.

Laura was glad that true to form Tom said very little on the journey. She didn't feel like talking. But when they turned into the station yard she asked, 'Tom, what are your intentions towards Amy Hannacott?'

'My intentions? Hah.' He muttered something to himself then, as he pulled Champion to a halt, he said, 'I was always sweet on Amy when we were young, but she married Eddie. He's been dead now some five years, and I know she misses him still. But when she's ready, I think she'll have me this time round.'

'I hope so,' Laura said softly.

'You won't change your mind and stay?'

'I have to get back to my family,' she told him, feeling affection for him well up. How wrong she'd been about him, and how right Brendan had been to trust him.

It started to rain as she went into the station and she was glad there was a small fire burning in the grate of the Ladies Waiting Room. The weather had really turned on its head as September approached, she thought. She was stretching her hands out to the fire when she heard the door open and felt a draught of cool air. She looked round. Brendan stood in the doorway, wet and dishevelled.

'Can I come in?' He barely waited for her nod and in two strides was taking hold of her hands. 'If you'd gone I would have taken the next train to London after you,' he said, his voice deep and his eyes bright with passion.

'Where have you been?' She hardly dared believe what he'd said.

'I went to see my father. I knew I could not talk about the future until I'd resolved the past and my position.' He kissed the tip of her nose.

'Um. And is everything resolved now?'

'Come and sit down.' He kept an arm round her, maintaining his contact. They settled side by side. 'I've mentioned a sister—but I had another. She contracted tuberculosis and was ill for many years. When I went to study medicine in Edinburgh I came across the work of a Dr Trudeau on TB. I wanted to try the new methods but my father refused. My sister died. I vowed to discover whether I was right, and there was a way to treat this disease, but my father wanted me to be a surgeon. I had a terrible quarrel with him.'

'I'm so sorry you lost your sister.' She clasped his hands in hers. 'It must have been a terrible time for your family.'

'I think that's what made my father and me fight. But now time has passed, and these past two days we have listened to each other. After losing one child he feared losing another, and

130

only wanted the best for me. He wouldn't try the new methods because he was afraid they would make my sister more ill. So,' he pulled her towards him, 'I have just been to Yorkshire, where I'm from. My family is well to do—my mother smuggled that silver coffee-pot down to me, she and I stayed in touch. If your shares are worth lots of money, that is yours, I don't want to touch it.'

Laura found she was smiling. 'Hold on a moment. Why would I think you're after my money.'

'Because I want us to get married.' He leaned forward and kissed her. After a while he pulled away, 'Did you say yes?'

'Mmmm? I think so . . .' He kissed her again.

This time she pulled away. 'And are you going to be a surgeon?'

'Would you mind if I decided not to? I was thinking of pioneering work in general medicine, maybe the London Hospital. But perhaps you want the status of a surgeon's wife?'

'Oh no. I was hoping you were going to say that. I'm afraid I'm going to have to carry on helping you.'

There was no further need for words as he pulled her close to him again so that she could feel his heart beating against her as their lips met again.